ANIMAL LAB

— A Novel —

Bob Zeidman

Swiss Creek Publications

Las Vegas, Nevada

Animal Lab

ISBN 978-0970227676

10 9 8 7 6 5 4 3 2 1

Book design by Carrie Zeidman

Printed in the United States of America

Freedom is a beautiful, fragile flower. It needs a sturdy pot in which to grow and constant watering. The pot is the law, the water is our diligence.

Dedication

This book is dedicated to my dad who instilled in me my strong moral framework and who believed in everything I did. If he were still with us, he would tell me I must write this book; it will be the best book ever written. This book is also dedicated to my mom who in her later years has become a good friend as she guides me into old age.

Contents

Introduction

Of course, one shouldn't yell "fire" in a crowded theater. But does it make sense to yell "fire" in a crowded theater that is actually on fire? That seems pointless. Everyone must see the flames and smell the smoke, right?

Some years ago, I was driving at rush hour on I880 near Oakland, California when I saw a flaming car on the side of the road under a bridge. Traffic was going at about 3 to 5 miles per hour right by it, only slightly slower than normal Bay Area rush hour speed. I had been approaching the slowdown for maybe 10 minutes, not sure what was causing it but seeing great plumes of smoke rising up from under the bridge. As I got closer, I could see occasional licks of bright yellow and red flames above the passing cars. When I finally got a good look, I thought, I should call the highway patrol! Then a more rational thought occurred to me: In all this time, of course someone had already called. Something in my brain said, what the heck. Maybe the highway patrol needs an update and I've got nothing else going on while stuck in traffic. I dialed 911, and the dispatcher thanked me for informing her about the situation and said she would call out a patrol car right away. Hanging up, I made myself a promise never to assume that others saw what I saw, no matter how obvious, or that if they saw it, that they took action.

Some years later I was at a coffee shop with a friend who is a doctor. As we talked, a shirtless man ran in and up to the counter and asked for a glass of water. "Quickly, please," he pleaded. He was in a panic, so the cashier got a cup, filled it with tap water, and gave it to him right away. The patrons of the crowded coffee shop all went silent, watching the man drink while a trickle of blood ran down his chest. "What happened?" I asked him.

"I was stabbed," the man replied.

I turned to my friend, the doctor, who shrugged and said something like "That's weird."

I took out my phone, dialed 911, explained the situation, ran to the street corner to note the crossroads to the dispatcher, and got assurance that a police car was on its way. The crowd in the coffee shop continued to stare and murmur. The crowd outside the coffee shop did the same.

Writing this book, I felt much the same way as I did in those incidents; I didn't know if anyone would care or if help would arrive. During the fits and starts of the writing process, I kept questioning if there was any point to writing about the things that were already going on around us. Would anyone care about my book if they didn't already care about the ideologies that were destroying the very values and principles of our civilization?

My previous book *Good Intentions* had been a warning about what was to come. Much more prophetic than I ever expected, many of my predictions, which I considered reductio ad absurdum, actually became reality within only a few years. In this book, I describe current events, in an allegory, but there's nothing in here that you can't see by walking the streets of any big city, joining any major corporation or institution, getting involved in politics, or watching the news. So I kept stopping my writing to doubt whether there was a point in pointing out the obvious.

But I kept thinking of many good friends—otherwise smart people—who promote writers, philosophers, and politicians who tell them they are bad people and can't be redeemed. They tell whites that they are inherently evil and must atone for the sins of all white people throughout history. They tell blacks that they are innately but understandably stupid and violent and need the help of others to succeed. They tell Hispanics that Americans hate them but then encourage them illegally into our country in droves. They tell Asians, many of whose families were brought here as cheap labor over a century ago, but who built great communities and businesses despite being shunned and interned in camps by government orders, that they have some invisible unfair advantage that allowed them to succeed. They tell Jews whose own parents and grandparents survived the greatest planned genocide in human history, and that faced anti-Semitism when they arrived here in America and yet built a thriving subculture and success in many industries and professions, that they are somehow "privileged" and should be ashamed of their success.

And so here am I yelling fire in a crowded theater. I just can't let myself be silent despite the risks of being cancelled. Of losing my business relationships and my career. The threat to the exceptional American experiment that has led so many people of all backgrounds to success and happiness, leads me to write what I've written here. I hope my point is well-expressed in this book. I hope that this book is fun enough and interesting enough that those who are oblivious to the problems around us will pick it up, enjoy it, and learn from it. I hope that people will take action to stop the destruction. I hope that one day people will look back at me, and others who are also crying out these warnings, and say, thank God we listened to them and put out the fire before our civilization burned to the ground.

Animal Lab

Chapter 1

Rizzo was the first to wake up. He looked around at the clean white walls and sparkling glass windows. Yesterday was cleaning day, and small teams of people in white coats had scrubbed and brushed and polished until everything was spotless. At least he thought it was yesterday. His mind was a little foggy, probably because he'd slept so late. Usually people began arriving at 8:00 AM, sometimes earlier. Sometimes people never left all night. But the movements and noises by 9:00 AM were always enough to wake him up.

He looked at the clock and squinted to read 11:17. Morning, he assumed, though the overhead fluorescent lights cast an even glow over everything all day, so it was hard to know. He supposed he could have woken up at night for some reason. Maybe his new treatments caused insomnia. That could be it. It's actually evening, which would explain why the place was empty.

Rizzo nudged Cagney beside him who stirred and rubbed his eyes. "What's up?" asked Cagney.

"Is it morning or night?" asked Rizzo.

"Huh?" replied Cagney. "Must be morning. The lights come on automatically in the morning. They're off at night unless some person comes into the room and there's no person in here."

"Why is that?"

"Hmmm... Good question. A holiday?"

"I thought we had some tests scheduled for today."

Beside them, Billie stirred. "What are you guys talking about?" she asked.

"There's no one here," said Cagney. He avoided looking at Billie. They'd once been a couple, but that was some time ago and then some things had happened that he didn't like to think about. They were both a bit uncomfortable around each other though they lived together still.

Billie began washing her face, still a little too groggy to take it all in. Rizzo looked over at Hickory, Dickory, and Doc and went over to rattle their cage.

"Wake up!" he said more than loudly enough to wake them. All three sat up at once, bewildered. "What?" they responded in unison.

"Look around," said Rizzo.

They did, then back at him. They didn't get it. Rizzo always thought of them as slow cousins. "No one's here," he explained. They stared at him blankly. "No one's here," he repeated.

"Hey!" Rizzo shouted into the open space. "Come get us out of here!"

"Out of here?"

Rizzo looked around and saw the mockingbird, Evan, doing what he does. Mocking.

At first, there was silence, and then a slow, plodding could be heard getting closer and louder. A large, dark, black body approached, casting a shadow over all of them. Julius opened the door. "Thank goodness for opposable thumbs," he said, as he often did. He was proud of this part of his anatomy, and it certainly came in useful at times like these, but Rizzo found these pronouncements tiresome. And boastful.

"Where are all the people?" asked Rizzo.

"Don't know" said Julius, rubbing the palms of his hands upward over his face and continuing over his head, smoothing the thick, dark black hair. "I'm just going around getting everyone out of their cages. The people are gone."

"We should have a meeting," said Rizzo. "Get everyone into the conference room in an hour."

"Will do," said Julius as he unlatched the cages and then lumbered on to the next room in the lab.

Chapter 2

The animals were gathered in the conference room. The mice Hickory, Dickory, and Doc occupied one seat. The rats Cagney and Billie were in another seat, but uncomfortably, turned slightly away from each other. The other rat, Rizzo, stood at the head of the table, on the tabletop. Julius, the chimpanzee, held the door as the others walked in.

Sniffer, the rabbit, sat in another chair, his nostrils pulsing rapidly in anticipation of… something. The guinea pigs Moonbeam, Alexander, and Pipsqueak sat in another chair, occasionally squeaking and shoving each other.

The older cat Milagra sat by herself on top of a filing cabinet, antisocial as usual. The younger cat Mayflower circled the desk, purring softly. Evan the mockingbird settled just out of reach of Milagra who eyed him menacingly, then closed her eyes.

Morgan, the dog, circled around the other animals, herding them into the room, tail wagging and not quite understanding what had happened. Actually none of them quite understood why the humans were missing, but hoped they would find out at the unusual meeting. Unusual, because animals didn't have meetings. Humans did. Sometimes one or two animals would attend. Obviously something had changed.

Other animals crowded into the lab, including several sheep, pigs, and monkeys, but left room for Arnold the tortoise, who was last to arrive, moving calmly, never hurried. Although Arnold was young in tortoise years, he was old in actual years, and the other animals gave deference to him.

When Arnold arrived, Rizzo cleared his throat, and the animals stopped their chatter to listen. "Fellow lab animals," he began and puffed up his chest a bit. "The humans are nowhere to be found. Dr. Muro and his staff seem to have vanished. We don't know what has happened to them, but as best we know, we are on our own now."

"On our own?" repeated Evan, but the others ignored him.

Gasps and murmurs and squeaks and growls rose up from the crowd.

"Please, please," shouted Rizzo above the din. "We can take care of ourselves. While we all have physical limitations, together we can accomplish anything." A phrase popped into Rizzo's brain. Had he heard it somewhere? Did a human plant it there as part of an experiment? No matter, it fit the situation. "In unity there is strength!"

The animals stared at Rizzo for a moment. Then, from the back of the room, Arnold's slow, deep, melodious voice repeated "In unity there is strength!" Then a few other animals repeated the catchy phrase. Within a few minutes, they were chanting it in unison.

After a few minutes, Rizzo waved his tiny hands to stop the chanting and continued. "We need order. We need a system. We need rules to live by to make this effort work."

"I heard about some animals in England," said Morgan excitedly, himself an English Terrier. "On a farm. They created a system called Animalism where all animals are equal. That sounds good to me."

The other animals made concurring sounds. "Sounds good to me, too," said one. "Equality—I like that," said another.

"I don't know," said Cagney. "We're not all equal. Some are big, some are small. Some are fast, some are slow."

"Some have opposable thumbs!" said Julius from the doorway, giving a thumbs-up sign with his hand.

"Yes, yes," said Cagney a bit dismissively. "We need a system that gives all animals an equal opportunity but recognizes our differences. A system that gives voice to all of us, but that respects our differences."

"We need a constitutional democratic republic," said Arnold. Though his voice was soft, it had a deep resonance that cut through all other chatter.

Following a prolonged silence, Rizzo asked, "OK. What's a constitutional democratic republic?"

"Every animal elects a representative by voting," said Arnold. Various expressions of approval sounded within the crowd. "And those representatives make the laws." More expressions of approval could be heard. "But first," he continued, "we must write a constitution—a written document declaring the basic rights of all animals—so that those rights cannot be taken away from us. Because as history has shown, many leaders will want more power and can only gain that power by diminishing everyone else's power. That must never be allowed."

"No, never!" Exclaimed a few of the animals.

"This sounds like a good plan," said Cagney. "Is there anyone opposed?"

"It won't work," came the voice of Milagra on the cabinet who had, until now, appeared to be sleeping.

"And why is that?" asked Cagney.

"Animal nature, that's all. But do as you wish." And then Milagra shut her eyes again.

"As you wish," repeated Evan.

Cagney hesitated for a moment, then continued, "We'll create a committee to write our constitution."

"We need a symbol," bellowed Arnold. "Something to represent our ideals. On a flag, so that everyone will know who we are and what we represent."

Cagney declared, "And a committee for that!"

And with that first conference was born Animerica.

Chapter 3

The committees were formed. The Constitution Committee consisted of the rats Rizzo, Cagney, and Billie along with Arnold the turtle and Julius, who was on every committee because of his ability to type, though the rats in particular were learning how to use keyboards.

After much discussion, debate, and arguing, a constitution was written. It consisted of some rules about elections and a legislature, executive, and a legal system. Perhaps most important, was that it included a short list of "The Seven Rights and Responsibilities" that the animals had drawn from various sources that they had actually learned from the humans over the years.

1. Every animal has the right to own and control property. Property may be physical or intellectual, with life being the most valuable property.
2. Property may be traded but not stolen. An animal convicted of stealing property will be required to compensate with its own property of equal value.
3. Animals are innocent of any crime until proven guilty in a court of law by a jury of its peers.
4. Animals have freedom of speech that cannot be denied by the government.
5. Animals have the right to defend their other rights by any means necessary as long as such defense does not deny the rights of any other animals.
6. Animals have the right to privacy.
7. All animals must be treated equally.

A flag was designed by the hummingbird Carrie Lee and was accepted by a unanimous vote of the animals. It consisted of 7 red stripes on a white background, representing the Seven Rights and Responsibilities, and a blue square in the upper left corner with 7 white paw prints from 7 different animals. The flag was placed at the front of the conference room, renamed Independence Room.

Julius wrote the Seven Rights and Responsibilities on a large whiteboard in Independence Room. A pledge was written by Rizzo. It was simple: "I pledge allegiance to the nation of Animerica and its Seven Rights and Responsibilities, as symbolized in its flag." It was proudly recited before each meeting in Independence Room, each animal raising its own voice above those of the others, or attempting to do so, in a display of pride in what they had created.

Chapter 4

The animals learned to harvest the crops for their meals and to feed themselves. The lab contained a large enclosed hydroponic garden area with an abundance of crops. Much of it was automated, but the animals needed to understand the robots and electronics and maintain them. Rizzo in particular took over much of the maintenance, learning the machinery and electronics but also teaching those others that had a knack for learning such things. He assigned work to each animal who applied for it, and created a monetary system for paying them.

The currency system was really rather simple. Animals traded goods and used currency to represent the trades. Just like the humans used to. Of course, the animals had no currency printing presses, but Rizzo discovered small packs of cards throughout the lab. These cards had numbers and symbols on them, though some cards had figures of people—royalty. Rizzo didn't know who they were, though they must have been important given their fancy dress. Some cards had the letter 'A,' which was obviously used for the smallest denomination of currency. Rizzo had scoured the entire lab, enlisting the help of the other smaller animals—rats, mice, Guinea pigs—to get into drawers and closets to search out all the packages of cards. He didn't ask the cats because Mayflower just didn't seem bright enough to understand and Milagra just wasn't trustworthy in his opinion. He knew that there were a few "mining expeditions" where animals would go out looking to discover unfound packs of cards, thus getting instantly rich, but figured there wasn't much he could do to prevent that.

The property was owned by the new Animerica government, but Rizzo considered that a temporary solution. As the animals took on jobs and earned their wages, the cages and rooms were auctioned off, except for a few rooms like Independence Room, that remained communal property, held by the government.

Cagney turned to philosophy, reading voraciously of the books stored on the computer, having taught himself to jump on the keypad to type into it. Billie also found an interest in philosophy and the animalities. They also rekindled, or perhaps just kindled, a respect for each other that became a good friendship and that eventually became a stronger bond—love or something akin to it. Whatever had happened between them in the past had been forgotten, or at least deeply buried.

An election was held and, to no one's surprise, Rizzo was elected president. A legislature was also created, and Cagney and Billie were leading members.

Things looked good for Animerica. The animals took pride in their work because their labor resulted in the improvement of their lives as opposed to the past, when humans forced them to perform tasks for seemingly no good reason. They had begun trading goods, they had an abundance of food, and most of them were happy, or at least pursuing happiness.

Chapter 5

Charlie Gordon finally had to come out of the closet. He had been in the supply closet for several weeks, living off a small supply of animal foods until it ran out one week ago. He was disheveled, confused, and very hungry. He unlocked the door and exited into the harsh light of the lab, his eyes blinking and tearing.

Charlie had been an assistant to Dr. Muro who ran the lab. Charlie had been considered "slow" by his fellow humans. He moved slowly and thought slowly, not able to grasp a lot of the concepts that most humans could—not even many of the concepts that the animals at the lab now could. He wandered the empty hallway, frightened, heading to the mouse habitats where he always felt comfort. He liked petting the soft mice fur and talking to them. As he approached the habitats, a few mice were mingling when they saw him coming and began whispering.

Charlie picked up a mouse and began petting it, feeling a bit less afraid. He started talking to it. "I missed you. Who's taking care of you now? What happened to everybody?"

"Hi Charlie," said the mouse after a while of petting. "Where have you been? Where are all the people?"

Charlie dropped the mouse onto the table. He was used to talking to them, not used to them talking back.

Evan the mockingbird had seen the whole thing, hanging out in the rafters. He quickly flew to Independence Room where Rizzo, Cagney, and Billie were laying out plans for the new government and the new society. "Human in Lab 16," he cawed. "Human in Lab 16'" he repeated then flew off back to Lab 16 where Charlie was standing, dumbfounded.

"Never heard an animal talk?" screeched Evan when he got back to Lab 16. "Never heard an animal talk?" he repeated.

Charlie backed away from Evan and the lab mice, into a corner, crouched, and began sobbing. Rizzo scurried into the room and up onto the desk in front of Charlie. Cagney and Billie came too. Evan retreated back to the rafters where he could observe silently.

"Charlie," said Rizzo, "it's OK. We're… your friends. Where have you been?"

Charlie hesitated. "In the closet."

"For how long?"

Charlie shrugged.

"Where is everyone? Dr. Muro? The researchers? The people?"

Charlie shrugged again. Rizzo thought Charlie might be in shock. Or it might be that his limited intelligence kept him from comprehending, or remembering, what had happened. He saw that Charlie was shivering from fear, and probably malnutrition. "Come with me, Charlie. We'll get you something to eat."

"Is that a good idea?" asked Billie.

Rizzo was taken aback. Billie rarely talked and almost never questioned him, or anyone. Maybe reading all those philosophy books has made her more outspoken. That would be a good thing.

"Why would that be?" asked Rizzo.

"He's animaliphobic. All humans are. You know how they treated us. He's capable of doing the same. We need to be wary."

"He's hungry and scared," replied Rizzo. "And Charlie never hurt any of us."

"I'm just saying it's in his nature. In his upbringing. We need to be wary. Humans held us in slavery."

Billie said a lot more, with very complicated words that Rizzo felt could have been said with much simpler words. Rizzo zoned out during her speech, but simply repeated, "Charlie never hurt any of us. I'm taking him for a meal." With that, he turned to Charlie. "Follow me, Charlie. We'll get you some good food. Things are different around here. We've made some changes."

Billie turned to Cagney. "I'm just worried," she said. "About the animals. About all of us. Humans kept us as pets. They bred us and used us for experiments. They ate us!"

"Charlie never hurt anyone. He's gentle." Said Cagney.

'But he's a human," replied Billie. "Can we really trust him?"

Cagney stared at Billie for a moment. Why had he never noticed how soft and shiny her fur is. And her voice is… soothing. Comforting. Even when talking about the threat of humans, it just sounded so… caring.

"Everything is so different now," said Billie. "I'm trying to understand it… I want to make sure things don't go back to the way they were. We have our freedom now. I don't want to lose it."

"I know," said Cagney. He moved toward her and nuzzled his face against hers. "It's all new. We'll figure it out." He backed off a bit, realizing that maybe he'd been a little too personal. But she moved back to him and nuzzled her face against his. "You'll figure it out," he said to her.

Chapter 6

After some days, Charlie became comfortable in Animal Lab. He had always been good to the animals, and they had always liked him. He was a simple, gentle man. He liked doing simple chores like cleaning cages and, well, mostly just cleaning things. He found comfort in making Animal Lab a better place for the animals, as he had when the humans had run the place. And he liked being useful and contributing.

One day, Julius came around to see Charlie. Julius had been avoiding Charlie and approached him cautiously as Charlie was sweeping a floor. Charlie saw Julius from the corner of his eye and froze.

"Nice thumbs," said Julius.

Charlie remained silent.

"I said, nice thumbs," repeated Julius. "I have two of my own." He held up both thumbs in front of Charlie's face. Charlie jerked back. "I'm just saying," continued Julius, "that we both have thumbs. Opposable ones. Very useful, wouldn't you say?" He pulled his hands from out of Charlie's face.

"Yes," said Charlie. "Very useful." Then after a moment, "Helps me hold the broom straight," and he held up the broom to show Julius.

"The other animals don't have them," said Julius. "Don't know how they get along without them."

"The monkeys have them," said Charlie quietly.

"Yes, the monkeys. But, you know, they're just monkeys."

"Yes. Just monkeys."

There was an awkward silence.

"You want to thumb wrestle.?" Asked Julius.

Charlie just looked at Julius but didn't answer.

"You know," continued Julius, "you grasp hands, count to three, then we each try to pin the other's thumb."

"Sure," said Charlie, a slight, goofy grin breaking out on his face. "That's what you want? You want to thumb wrestle?"

Julius put out his right hand, thumb up. Charlie hesitantly grabbed it, his thumb also at attention. "One, two, three," said Julius, and pinned Charlie's thumb. Charlie giggled.

"Try it again?" asked Julius.

"Sure," said Charlie, and they repeated the thumb war, with the same outcome.

This became a regular thing for the two of them over the next weeks. For Charlie, it was a way to bond with the closest thing to a human at Animal Lab. For Julius, it was a way to convince himself that he really was the most capable animal at the lab. And still had the advantage of his opposable thumbs.

Chapter 7

"Equality," said Billie.

"Diversity," said Cagney.

"They're not mutually exclusive."

"But which do we prioritize?"

"Which did the humans put first. No doubt we should do the opposite."

A murmur was growing outside their lab, but they hardly noticed it at first. As it grew louder, they found themselves straining their voices to hear each other. They turned to the hallway and heard growling among the murmuring. And some surprisingly loud peeps.

A black shadow fell over them. Above, Evan was circling. "Trouble," he said. "Trouble," he repeated. He flew out the door, Cagney racing behind him, Billie behind him.

As they rounded a corner, there were animals lining the hallway, moving slowly toward the sounds, which grew louder as they got closer.

"Out of the way!" shouted Billie.

Rounding another corner, the crowd thickened.

"Out of the way!" shouted Billie again.

Cagney had an easier time keeping up with Evan, while Billie fell behind. They rounded another corner where the entrance to one of the labs was blocked by a mass of animals. Evan flew over them. Cagney easily squeezed between and under them.

In one corner of the room, Milagra was hissing and mewing, swinging her paw under a cabinet, claws extended, her loose flabby skin pulsating with each swing. "Come out!" she screamed. There was a small trail of blood leading under the cabinet.

Behind the cabinet was a peeping sound, much louder than Cagney imagined a peeping sound could be from an animal.

"What's going on here?" Cagney demanded as Billie caught up and entered the room.

Milagra turned to look at Billie and then at the crowd as if she had no idea a crowd had gathered; with a look like it was no one else's business but her own. Milagra turned back to the cabinet and took another swipe.

"What's going on?" Billie demanded. The crowd went silent. Milagra turned to look at Billie.

"She took my food," said Milagra. "Sniffer. She's under there. She took the food I'd been saving."

From under the table, Sniffer's small voice came out in a trickle, like the trickle of her blood on the floor. "I found it," she said. "I didn't know it was hers."

"Like hell," said Milagra. "I wrote my name on it."

"I don't read too well," said Sniffer meekly. The glow of her rabbit eyes shone from under the cabinet.

There was a silent pause, while everyone waited for Billie to make a statement. She had become the philosopher king in the lab. She read more than anyone, knew more than anyone.

"Look at you," said Billie, motioning to Milagra. You certainly get enough to eat." She paused for effect. "Let her have your food."

Billie turned to the crowd. "We don't hoard here. We have abundance. We won't be like the humans. Animals take care of each other. Share with each other. We're creating a great, new society. We trade, we barter, but we do it with compassion. On a level playing field. Don't anyone forget that!"

Billie turned back to Milagra and Sniffer. "Come on out, Sniffer," she said.

Milagra was silent, her eyes shifting back and forth between Billie in front of her and Sniffer under the cabinet.

"I'm afraid," said Sniffer.

Billie noticed Julius in the doorway, peering over the heads of the other animals.

"Julius," commanded Billie, "Take Milagra out of here."

Julius shrugged, stepped over the other animals, and picked up Milagra who took a couple swipes at him, hissing. He ignored her; his tough skin could withstand her claws. She wriggled and twisted her body violently as only a cat can do, but Julius held on, once again admiring his opposable thumbs, as he took her out of the room.

Sniffer came out from under the cabinet. "Thank you, Billie."

Billie nodded, turned toward the door, and began walking out. Cagney accompanied her. "You were great," he said. His admiration for her grew every day. And his passion for her.

As they walked out the door, Rizzo came running in. "What happened?" he asked.

"Where were you?" asked Billie and she continued down the hall.

Rizzo looked after her, puzzled.

A buzz grew among the animals that gave way to soft cheering that grew louder. Billie and Cagney didn't look back.

Chapter 8

The next day, Sniffer was found dead. Eaten. Her torn carcass was strewn about the lab where she had been attacked by Milagra the day before. Blood in Rorschach patterns on the tile floor. Charlie found her when he went to clean up.

Cagney had called an emergency meeting of the legislature in Independence Room. Rizzo strolled in—he hadn't been invited. He took a seat in the back. The roles of the three branches of government had not been fully defined, so maybe this was a legislative problem, but still he thought he should have been informed. But their new society was still figuring things out, so he didn't press it. People had more important things on their minds.

"… bad thing" said Cagney to the assembled legislators.

"Not just a bad thing," chimed in Billie, "but unacceptable. Completely unacceptable. No one can be allowed to take the life of an animal." She paused dramatically and went from face to face, pausing at each face. "Especially a small, innocent one. A defenseless one." A tear came to her eye. "One of the better ones."

The animals nodded and murmured to each other.

"What do we do?" asked Hickory.

"What's the procedure for such a thing?" asked Dickory.

"What do the rules say?" asked Doc.

There was more murmuring. Cagney looked to Billie for an answer.

"We're still figuring all these things out," she said. "We're putting together the rules as we go." That didn't sound the way she meant it. "Great rules," she added. "Fair rules. Especially for the innocents. Protecting the vulnerable."

The animals seemed to like that. Fairness was… well, fair. Everyone wanted fairness.

"We need to put together a fair trial." Billie had latched onto the word "fair." She believed wholeheartedly in fairness, but it had the added benefit of appealing to everyone. Who would argue with fairness?

"First we appoint a jury of Milagra's peers." That was the first time anyone had actually spoken Milagra's name, though everyone was convinced of her guilt.

"Then we appoint lawyers. One for Sniffer." The crowd sniffed. A few mournful warbles and coos. "And one for Milagra." There was restless shifting and soft coughing at the mention of Milagra's name.

"And Arnold will preside over the trial of course, as the judge," added Cagney. Billie started to speak, but the crowd immediately made approving cooing noises and heads nodded. "We all know him," said Cagney. "We all trust him," he added. Cagney turned to Billie, "And he's fair."

Billie didn't seem pleased but then looked at the crowd. "I was about to suggest Arnold," said Billie to the crowd. "Excellent choice." She then turned, hopped off the table, and walked quietly out the door, leaving Cagney to handle the other matters like making the motions, approving the motions, going through the other items on the agenda, and closing the meeting.

Chapter 9

"It's imperative that we create a just and fair society!"

"Of course," said Cagney. He noticed how Billie's nose twitched faster when she got emotional speaking about a subject, and these days that subject was politics. Her fine whiskers also twitched rapidly. And sometimes a cute little squeak would come out at the end of a sentence. She had found her passion. And it was attractive. Why had he not noticed that before? Maybe because she had never spoken so intensely before. Or spoken much at all, actually.

"Of course," he repeated. "But how do we define a just and fair society?"

"How can you not just know?" she said. "Fair is fair. It's equality. It's things that… well, everyone knows what fairness is." She stopped for a moment in thought. "No society can surely be flourishing and happy, of which the far greater part of the members are poor and miserable."

"Yes, OK," he said. "But the question is how to make sure that none of the animals are poor and miserable. That's where we disagree."

"It's easy," she said. "From each according to his ability, to each according to his needs. It's tried and true. Have you been reading the books I've been leaving for you?"

"Yes," he said, a little annoyed at the condescending tone. He recognized that Billie grasped abstract concepts faster than he did. He was amazed at her ability to absorb ideas quickly that required a lot of his time and concentration. And some of these ideas were so complex, so involved, that he was embarrassed to admit that he still didn't get them all. But he wanted to keep up with her. Her energy was infectious. And very attractive. "It is not from the benevolence of the butcher, the brewer, or the baker that we expect our dinner, but from their regard to their own interest. We shouldn't just go about 'making things fair.' We need to set up a system of trade. And enforce rules of fairness. But light rules, not heavy restrictions."

"I can't believe you would bring up a butcher. The humans that slaughtered animals for food. How could you bring that into our conversation?" Billie's ears were vertical and rigid. Her whiskers pulled back sharply.

"I'm sorry… really. I was quoting a source… I wasn't thinking." Cagney blushed but it probably wasn't visible under his smooth coat of gray fur. But Billie could certainly smell it. He looked down, then meekly replied "If an exchange between two parties is voluntary, it will not take place unless both believe they will benefit from it."

"OK," said Billie a bit softer. She did notice Cagney's embarrassment and, well, it attracted her. A vulnerable male rat. The idea was new to her, but she liked it. "But rats are the only animals that make bargains; no other animal does this."

"What about our bone exchange program for dogs?" asked Cagney.

"A program designed by rats," said Billie. "It's successful because it was designed by rats. But the dogs can't take care of themselves. That's why we're needed. To make our society fair."

Billie's and Cagney's noses shot into the air, sniffing rapidly.

"It's just me," said Rizzo as he walked around the corner. He had on a red cap that he wore as a symbol of his leadership. Sometimes the other animals had difficulty differentiating the rats, and Charlie the human couldn't seem to do it at all. So he had Carrie Lee make him a simple red hat. "I hear you talking about government and fairness using all these highfalutin words."

Billie and Cagney looked at each other. "What's 'highfalutin' mean?" asked Cagney.

Rizzo chuckled. "I just mean you're talking about all these things—which is great because someone needs to do that—I just have so many things to take care of that I don't have time for philosophical discussions. I'm kind of jealous."

A large shadow suddenly engulfed the three of them. They looked up to see Evan descending. "Another human," he said. "Another human in Lab 62." Then he flew off. Rizzo, Cagney, and Billie scampered off to Lab 62.

A young human girl, about 6 years old, stood quietly in the corner, looking straight ahead but not frightened. Just blankly. She was dirty and her clothes were worn and soiled. And torn in places, though Rizzo remembered that some human girls liked torn clothes for some reason, so maybe they started out that way.

Evan flew in front of her face and just a foot away, flapping his wings to hover in place. "Another human," he said. "Another human; how many are out there?" The girl didn't seem disturbed by the bird; maybe curious. Or maybe in shock. No one knew what the humans had been through, or anything about what had happened outside the lab, but surely something had happened.

"Go away, Evan. You're scaring her." Evan flew back to the rafters to observe silently. "Someone get Charlie," shouted Rizzo to the crowd that had gathered. Julius had been watching from the doorway. He ran away and came back in a few minutes with Charlie.

"Take her, Charlie," said Rizzo.

"Where?" asked Charlie.

"Make a place for her. Make her comfortable. I have a feeling we'll be getting more human guests. Set aside Lab 42 for the humans. Can you do that?"

"I guess so," said Charlie. He walked softly over to the girl, reached out, and gently took her arm. She followed silently, staring at all the animals in the lab as they walked out to Lab 42.

Over the next few weeks, other humans started showing up. There were children, many dirty and disheveled and nonverbal, either unable to speak or not having learned to speak. They just showed up, possibly having wandered into the lab from the street somehow, though the heavy doors, electronic controls, and complex security measures made it seem impossible for anything to get in or out. And the animals were not in a hurry to understand what was going on outside the lab or in the rest of the world.

A few adults showed up, too. Archie Brock had been seen getting treatment at the lab, along with the animals, but no one knew what for, including Archie. Sheila Corinth had been the wife of one of the researchers, but she also had no recollection and little understanding of what had happened or how she ended up there.

Most of the humans would be considered to have below average human intelligence levels before Day 1, as the animals had started counting days. Rizzo began to wonder if that had something to do with why they survived whatever had happened. And what did happen to the humans? There still were no answers.

Rizzo worked with Charlie, Archie, and Sheila to set aside rooms for the humans to live. And classrooms for the children. And play areas, of course. He wanted to integrate them into the new animal society—after all, humans are animals too—but he wanted to take it slowly. It was going to be difficult to bring animals and humans together. It was a whole new world with challenges that no animal had ever faced before. And many of the animals were uncomfortable with the humans around. Especially Billie. Which he understood. His job as president was to keep everyone calm as they worked out solutions.

Chapter 10

The day for Milagra's trial had finally come. The room called Justice Room was turned into a courtroom. Milagra sat on one side, flattened in the chair, eyes going back and forth, ready to shoot out onto the floor and out the door. Except that Julius sat next to her, hand hovering over her, ready to slam it down, if necessary, to keep her there. Anyway, where would she go? Any escape would be temporary because there were few places to hide in the lab where she wouldn't eventually be caught.

Sheila sat next to her, acting as her attorney. Sheila had gone to law school before marrying, having kids, and raising them. She was concerned that having a human lawyer might not be great optics for Milagra in front of the all-animal jury, but none of the animals wanted to represent her. They had all seen or heard from someone who had seen Milagra's attack on Sniffer. Most already knew she was guilty but were eager to test out their new judicial system. It was a novelty for them—bringing fairness to the animal world where previously only the strong survived, and might made right.

Representing the government was the dog Morgan. It seemed appropriate to appoint him though he didn't know much about the law or the animal legal system. Truth be told, there was no animal legal system as yet, so this would be a precedent-setting case.

Arnold slowly took his place at the front of the room and settled in for a long trial. Arnold was slow but his mind was quick. And he had lots of patience to listen for long periods, weigh the facts. Of course his role was as judge, so the decision was not up to him but rather up to the jury. But he needed to keep things on track. To prepare, he had read an entire library of legal texts and case law. He moved slowly but read quickly and absorbed everything.

The jury of Milagra's peers sat to the side, trying to sit still but the mice, rats, Guinea pigs, and rabbits on the jury had a hard time sitting still. They fidgeted in their seats and were distracted by the other animals in the gallery in the back who were whispering and peeping and growling, creating a quiet cacophony not unlike an orchestra quietly tuning its instruments before a concert. Television cameras carried the trial throughout the laboratory, and most animals were gathered around the TV screens.

Arnold called the court to order, banging his ball-peen hammer on the table in lieu of a gavel. The crowd quieted.

Sheila began opening arguments. "Ladies and gentlemen." She suddenly got uncomfortable. She had rehearsed her speech many times to herself, but now she felt the stares of dozens of tiny eyeballs. She started questioning herself. Do they refer to themselves as "ladies and gentlemen"? Or do they use some other term. Was that somehow insulting? Or respectful, as she meant it to be? The pause was growing uncomfortable, and the crowd began murmuring.

"Is something wrong?" asked Arnold.

"Sorry, your honor… able tortoise. Sir."

"Please continue, advocate Sheila. This is new for all of us."

Sheila nodded and cleared her throat nervously. "What we want is justice. Truth and justice. But truth is never absolute. Who among you knows the absolute truth? We are still trying to understand what happened on Day 0 and then Day 1 that created the world in which we live." She again paused, worried that a human discussing Days 0 and 1 might be inappropriate. Rules in this society were changing and she sometimes broke protocols of propriety without knowing. She realized quickly that her hesitation was worse than her concerns, so she quickly continued before Arnold had a chance to question her again.

"In court, we never get to the truth, but we do get to reasonable truth. And only reasonable proof of guilt can… or should be used to convict a person… I mean an animal… of a crime, especially one as serious as murder. In a fair, just society, one is innocent until proven guilty." She emphasized the word "proven" and paused, this time for dramatic effect.

"In the case before you, the things we know are that Sniffer, may she rest in peace, was taking food from Milagra. The day before Sniffer's death, Milagra fought with Sniffer. Milagra was angry. She had worked hard for her food. If Milagra had intended to kill Sniffer, she could have done it then. But she didn't. Like the rest of us, Milagra has sworn to uphold the rules of our society.

"The next day, Sniffer was sadly found dead. Milagra was nowhere nearby. No one saw Milagra at the scene or communicating with Sniffer. You will hear from Milagra that she was napping the entire day, upset about what had happened the previous day.

"In a fair and just society, we convict someone only when we have the facts. We have no facts in this case. Nothing that puts Milagra at the scene, nothing that proves that Milagra did anything wrong. You must disregard your feelings and rely on facts. In the absence of facts, such as in this case, you must acquit Milagra."

Sheila paused and looked into the eyes of each animal on the jury. Many turned away when she looked at them. Not a good sign among human juries, but with animal juries? This was all so new. Then she quietly sat back down.

Morgan trotted up to the front and looked at the jury. He fought hard to stop his tail from wagging. "Members of the jury," he started in his low howling voice. "Milagra is a cat. Cats eat small rodents. It's in their nature."

"Objection, your honor," shouted Sheila as she stood.

"I'm going to give a lot of leeway for opening arguments, Sheila, so I'm overruling the objection. You can address it when appropriate during the trial."

Morgan's tail began wagging and he quickly had to focus to stop it. "We know that Milagra did not 'scratch' Sniffer, as her defense council claimed. We all know that Milagra viciously attacked Sniffer. There was blood on the floor. Milagra physically wounded Sniffer and might have killed her if a crowd of witnesses hadn't shown up."

Sheila stood to object but stopped halfway, paused, and sat back down. She knew Arnold would overrule, but at least the jury saw her make the attempt.

"Milagra's human counsel has said that we need to have facts to find the truth." He emphasized the word 'human.' "The facts are that Milagra attacked Sniffer, wounded her gravely, and was the only one who had the motive and anger to kill her. Those are the facts. And the truth is that Milagra is a murderer who must be punished." Morgan strutted back to his place at the side of the table.

The trial was short. Morgan repeated what everyone knew about the fight the day before Sniffer's murder. Sheila reiterated that they must not convict without proof, evidence. Sheila considered putting Milagra on the stand to testify, but Milagra was a testy and irate animal, and the jury, most of which were small rodents, would probably not sympathize with her.

Then came the short closing arguments. Morgan went first: "I reminded you of the facts that you already knew. No one else had threatened Sniffer. No one else had attacked Sniffer. No one else had a motive. Put one and one together and you get two. Milagra murdered Sniffer. Period."

Then came Sheila: "What happened the day *before* Sniffer's murder is irrelevant. What we must know is what happened the day *of* Sniffer's murder. And the fact is… we just don't know. You cannot convict someone based on things you do not know. Milagra must be found innocent."

The jury deliberated for only a short time, about an hour, before coming back with a verdict of guilty. The crowd in Justice Room, as well as most of those throughout the lab, let out a roaring cheer.

Arnold brought down his hammer hard, several times. The crowd in Justice Room very slowly quieted down with each slam of the hammer on the table.

"This is all new to us," said Arnold. "It will all take some getting used to." Arnold surveyed the room full of confused eyes. "Justice requires proof, and the prosecutor provided no proof. Therefore I take it upon myself to correct the judgment, as is within my power. The defendant is declared not guilty."

Milagra had been mostly confused during the proceedings, constantly planning an all-but-impossible escape. Milagra's heart had started pounding at the declaration of her guilt and she had been ready to run for it when Arnold had spoken up. Her mind was still racing, trying to understand what happened, when Sheila placed her hand on Milagra's back and ran it down her fur. Milagra stood up—she never liked being petted. But then she loosened her taught muscles and let out a purr as the result sank in.

Billie was in the back of the room when she heard the jury verdict and Arnold's annulment of it. Furious, she ran out of the room to find Cagney.

"Did you hear?" asked Billie.

"I just saw it on TV," said Cagney. He really was confused by the law and wasn't sure what Billie's reaction would be. Was this a miscarriage of justice or was this a correction of injustice?

"The people spoke, and then a single person who believes he is wiser than the common folk decides to take matters into his own claws."

Obviously Billie was angry, so Cagney chimed in support. "Yes, a miscarriage of justice. Horrible. But what can be done?"

"What can be done? We run the legislature. We can correct this."

"We can?"

"Of course! When justice is not being served, we'll serve it."

Over the next few days, Cagney, at the behest of Billie, called an emergency meeting of the legislature. She argued her case strenuously and took a vote. That legislature ordered that Milagra be leashed until such time as the legislature determines that she has repented for her crime.

Chapter 11

"God could be a giant chimpanzee."

"But he's not. He's a man… a human."

"How do you know?"

"I've seen the pictures."

"Pictures? They have cameras in heaven? Do they post them on social media or are they still printing them on paper?"

"I mean the paintings. Like on the ceiling in that big chapel in Rome. God is a human with long white hair and beard. A big guy. But a nice guy. Wise and all-knowing. He floats around in the sky and looks down at everyone, trying to get them to do the right things. You know… be good people."

"And good animals, right? So maybe he's an animal. You've never seen him, right?"

"No, except in the paintings."

"But he never came to you and said, Charlie, I'm God. How do you do?" Julius stuck out his hand to Charlie.

Charlie laughed. "No, of course not. I'm not crazy."

"OK, so you don't know." Said Julius. "He could be a chimpanzee."

"I like to think he's a man. A big, nice man who will protect us from bad things."

"Or a big chimpanzee who will protect us from bad things. Like me." Julius stood erect, proudly, with the makeshift policeman's cap on his head. All of the animals had chosen jobs and Julius had chosen security. Since he was big and strong, and had opposable thumbs, he reasoned, he should be in charge of security. Carrie Lee had made this cool cap for him. But since everything was going so smoothly, and animals tended to be honest, there wasn't really much for him to do. So he hung out as Charlie swept the floors of the Guinea pig quarters. Charlie generally kept things clean in the lab. After all, that's what he did BA (before animals), so it made sense for him to do it now.

"Or a tortoise," said Charlie. "A wise tortoise."

Julius thought about it for a minute, envisioning Arnold flying around in the sky with long white hair and a beard. He chuckled. "I guess so," he said.

Charlie chuckled. "Or a Guinea pig."

They both simultaneously imagined a flying Guinea pig with long white hair flying around, squeaking, and peering down on them. They both started laughing out loud. It just seemed funny.

Pipsqueak the Guinea pig had been curled up in the corner of the room, on the floor under a cabinet, trying to sleep, but their chitter-chatter had kept him awake. He was supposed to be working in the farm but decided he'd rather nap. He had been getting annoyed at their gabbing, but that last remark made him angry.

Neither Julius nor Charlie had noticed Pipsqueak in the corner. As they talked, Charlie had been sweeping the floor and pushed his broom into the corner, jabbing Pipsqueak.

"What the...?" squeaked Pipsqueak.

Charlie and Julius kept debating about God while Charlie kept jabbing Pipsqueak with the broom. He felt something in the corner under the cabinet and instinctively tried to dislodge it. Pipsqueak kept squeaking and the jabbing got increasingly painful. Pipsqueak finally ran from under the cabinet and screamed at them. Julius stopped talking.

"But if there's a God, he must set the rules, right?"

"Wait a minute, Charlie, did you hear something?"

"No." They both went silent and suddenly could hear Pipsqueak's tiny yelling.

"What are you trying to do to me? I'm down here and you're jabbing me. Ignoring me. Trying to kill me?"

Charlie looked down, straining to hear. "Sorry, Pip," he said. Never really good with words, he didn't know what to say. He wasn't really sure what had happened. He just knew that Pipsqueak was upset about something. Charlie heard a lot of sounds, but they didn't all make sense to him. He knew the animals could speak—something that took some getting used to still—but while he could understand some, like Julius, others were hard to understand.

After a minute or so of angry squeaks, Pipsqueak scampered out of the room. Charlie looked at Julius, who understood most of the animals better than he did.

"Don't worry about it," said Julius. "He's upset. But it was a mistake. You said you were sorry. He'll get over it."

Chapter 12

Pipsqueak found Rizzo in Lab 221, walking on the desktops, reviewing the equipment. One of the computers was turned on, and Rizzo went back and forth from the equipment to the computer, stepping carefully on the keyboard to take notes. Pipsqueak climbed onto the table and watched Rizzo for a while, unnoticed.

"Mr. President," Pipsqueak finally shouted.

Rizzo turned around. "Pip. What are you doing here? I thought you'd be at the farm."

"Something just happened that you need to be aware of."

"At the farm?"

"No, in the Guinea pig quarters. I was just there minding my own business…"

"Why weren't you at the farm?"

"I was just attacked."

At that moment, Billie had walked in to talk to Rizzo. "Attacked?" she asked.

"Yes," said Pipsqueak, turning to her.

"That can't stand. This is a place of peace. Tell me what happened."

Pipsqueak turned his back to Rizzo to face Billie. "Charlie attacked me with his broom. He just started jabbing me for no reason. I kept crying out for him to stop but he wouldn't."

"That's unacceptable," said Billie, obviously truly concerned.

"You look OK, though," said Rizzo.

"And they were laughing at me, laughing at all Guinea pigs actually," added Pipsqueak, still looking at Billie.

"They?" asked Billie. "Who?"

"Julius and Charlie. They were both insulting Guinea pigs in the Guinea pig quarters.

"This needs to be fixed!" said Billie adamantly.

"What needs to be fixed?" asked Rizzo.

"Seriously?" asked Billie, staring down Rizzo. "You need to ask that? This is a place of peace. We're not going to tolerate insults, discrimination, hate speech!"

"OK," said Rizzo. He wasn't really intimidated by Billie. She knew a lot of words, but she got little done. She and Cagney did a lot of reading and talking, but very little work. At first their discussions were interesting, but after a while they got tiresome. He figured if they stayed to themselves, debated politics and philosophy, and caused no harm to anyone, then he'd leave them be.

"I'm going to take care of this," she said.

Pipsqueak puffed himself up and smiled.

"OK," said Rizzo. "Whatever you think is necessary." He was just glad to get her out of his hair. She was always upset about some abstract concept and just wasn't as pleasant to be around as she had been before Day 1. Rizzo turned back to his computer and equipment.

"Humans," Billie said disdainfully as she jumped off the table onto the floor. "And near-humans." She exited the lab, Pipsqueak behind her.

Chapter 13

"Hey, man" said Julius as he entered the room and encountered Charlie sweeping.

Charlie looked up. "Hey, monkey."

Julius stared at Charlie for a long moment, then broke into a big, toothy ape grin. The kind that actually had begun to embarrass him. He'd been working on making it more subtle, but it was hard. Harder, at least than the delicate movements of his opposable thumb.

Charlie smiled and started giggling. "You want to thumb wrestle again, right? You just want to break off my thumbs so that you're the only one around here that's got 'em."

"Me and the monkeys," said Julius, laughing.

As Billie came down the hallway, Pipsqueak trailing behind her, she could hear Charlie and Julius talking and laughing. The sound made her angrier. She rounded the corner into the Guinea pig quarters just as they were coming out. A few animals were going about their business in the hallway, but they slowed, sensing something.

"What the hell did you just do?" she shouted up at Charlie.

Charlie cowered a bit. "I just cleaned up the Guinea pig quarters. I'm heading over to the rat quarters now." He thought maybe she was upset that he hadn't prioritized the rat quarters.

"This is a place of peace and tolerance!"

The animals in the hallway stopped to listen. A few more came out of the rooms.

"Yes," said Charlie cautiously, as if it were a question rather than a statement. He still didn't understand.

"No one species can hurt another species. Do you understand that?"

"Of course," said Charlie, a quiver in his voice.

"You attacked this animal," she said, pointing to Pipsqueak now proudly puffed out into a 3-inch ball of fur.

"No I didn't."

Julius stepped forward, standing erect, looking down at tiny Billie. "No he didn't," said Julius.

"They both did," squeaked Pipsqueak,

"Huh?" said Julius.

"You attacked him with the broom after insulting Guinea pigs." Said Billie.

"No," said Julius chuckling. "We…"

"You attacked him," repeated Billie. "You laughed at him then and you're laughing at him now."

Julius paused, now confused himself.

"This is a place of peace, of tolerance. There will be no discrimination! At all. Do you understand me?"

"Yes, ma'am," said Charlie.

She looked at Julius. "And you, our security chief. Why aren't you protecting the innocent rather than siding with attackers?"

Julius started to speak, "But…"

Billie screamed, "Peace and tolerance, get it? No discrimination! No violence!" She turned to walk down the hallway, Pipsqueak following as the crowd of animals watched the procession. "Especially from humans," she added. "Or near-humans."

Chapter 14

Rizzo had been mostly absent from the public eye for months. His focus had been on practical matters to keep their new animal society functioning and prosperous, with opportunities for all of the animals. He set up committees to oversee a new educational system, business relations, labor standards, lab security, finances, distribution of health supplies, and complaints. He believed in keeping a light touch, but felt that guidelines were required, and in some cases, for example where animal safety was concerned, standards were required.

He had been wandering around the lab, looking at all of the electronic equipment, trying to figure out how it all worked. He had been reading engineering books, but they weren't like philosophy. They required building on previous knowledge, which meant starting from the basics, books like *Just Enough Electronics to Impress Your Friends and Colleagues!* You could just pick up a book on philosophy and start reading it and think, that makes a lot of sense. Or that's really stupid. But with engineering, you needed to start with mathematics. And then first principles. There were rules. And then you tested your work by actually building things and if they worked, you were right. If they failed, you had done something wrong. There were absolutes, as opposed to philosophy where everyone could claim to be right and there was no way of testing it. Rizzo liked rules and absolutes and certainty. He could handle uncertainty, but it drained him. Mentally and emotionally. And frightened him a little, if he were to be truthful with himself, because philosophy could uplift you or take you down the road to destruction, but you didn't know until you got where you were going.

One day it occurred to him that all of the wonderful equipment in the lab could certainly find some use in their new society, but he didn't need to figure it out by himself. There were many great minds and out-of-the-cage thinkers in their new society. The government could offer incentives to put the equipment to good use. There could be competitions for funding. The government could solicit proposals, and the best proposals would get funded. Maybe the lab equipment could be used for medical purposes. Or for improving the yield of the farms. New sources of energy. Or for entertainment. He had been thinking too much of him being the leader of this new society and so he needed to think of everything and do everything. But he learned that a great leader leads. Encourages. Makes opportunities. A leader's actions inspire others to dream more, learn more, do more and become more. He'd read that somewhere, and it made a lot of sense.

He would call it the Inspiration Project He would set up a committee to oversee it. The legislature was required to approve all allocations of funds and all committees, but he could always slip a new committee into their review process and they would approve it without much debate. The legislature was concerned mostly with abstract principles and didn't bother much with practical matters, so they left that to him. As long as everything was running smoothly, and there was enough food and shelter for everyone, the legislature spent its sessions arguing philosophy and approving committees and funds, and that was OK with Rizzo.

A year had passed since Day 1. Year 2 had begun, and elections were planned at the end of the year. Rizzo had so much work ahead, but he didn't want to spend time campaigning because it took so much time away from the real work. Anyway, he was popular among the animals as their standard of living had risen significantly from the days when they lived in cages. He knew that reelection was a certainty, so he focused on his programs and took great pride in the progress of Animerica. Anyway, who would challenge him in an election?

In Lab 7, a discovery was made that would change things.

Chapter 15

Alarm bells started ringing throughout the lab. It was about 3 AM.

Julius and Charlie had rigged up a system to warn of emergencies. They had set up pull switches in the lab. There were already emergency switches that activated the lab alarm system, but they also set off sprinklers. Most were out of reach of the animals and required a strength to pull that the smaller animals just didn't have. Also, it was believed that these switches notified authorities in the outside world, something the animals decided they didn't want. The animals still didn't know what was happening in that world and were afraid to find out, at least until they were prepared for it.

The switches that Julius and Charlie installed were at all height levels. The higher-level switches took more strength to pull. The lower-level switches required a small animal to jump onto it to pull it down. And they were all marked in colors and patterns that all the animals could recognize.

Julius quickly swung into action. Literally. A light blinked above his bed, telling him which alarm had been pulled and where it was located. He grabbed his security cap that he kept by his bed and ran, jumped, and swung around the hallways toward the pulled emergency switch. He arrived there first, to find Dickory crouched in a corner, head down, shivering. In the opposite corner was a small lump of bloody flesh.

"Dickory, what happened?"

Animals were trickling in, but staying out of the room, crowding into the hallway. Dickory was silent. Head down. Shivering.

Rizzo pushed his way through the crowd, rubbing the sleep from his eyes. He looked up at Julius, then across to Dickory, then walked to the bloody lump and began sniffing. "It's Hickory," he said softly.

Murmuring started among the crowd.

Julius turned to Rizzo. "He's not talking."

"He's in shock," replied Rizzo. "Let's take him somewhere quiet. Can you pick him up?"

"You think he did this?" asked Julius.

Rizzo looked at the lifeless lump and tried to imagine how Dickory could have done this to Hickory. Or why. It was hard to imagine. But then again, rodents could be vicious when provoked, even mice. Or when they believed they were being provoked.

Julius cupped his hand lightly around the shivering Dickory and picked him up. "Where to?" he asked.

"My quarters," said Rizzo.

Julius walked slowly out of the room toward Rizzo's quarters, gently cupping Dickory in his hands. Just then, Charlie showed up outside the room, behind the crowd of animals, positioning himself to see what was going on inside.

"Charlie," said Rizzo, "come on in."

Charlie stepped over the animals into the lab.

"Don't touch anything. And keep everyone out."

"Everyone out," said Charlie though all of the animals were already keeping their distance outside the room.

Billie came running into the room.

"Everyone out," said Charlie to Billie.

Billie looked up at him, then back at Rizzo. "What's going on?" she asked.

"Another killing," said Rizzo, and then he pointed toward the lifeless lump in the corner.

Billie made a face. "And where was Julius going?"

"To my quarters. He has Dickory. He's pretty shaken up. I want to talk to him."

"You think he did it?"

"I don't know. Could be. I doubt it. But I don't know."

"I'm going with you to talk to him."

"Billie, hold off. Let me talk to him first. One on one."

"Male to male?"

"Sure. I just want him relaxed. He's pretty upset."

"I'm going," said Billie.

Rizzo sighed and walked through the crowd toward his quarters, Billie following behind but then catching up to walk side-by-side. She walked behind no one.

Chapter 16

Julius uncupped his hands on the table and gently placed Dickory in front of Rizzo and Billie. "Do you need me here?" he asked. "For security."

"We don't need you," said Billie brusquely.

"I think we're OK," said Rizzo. "Why don't you go back to the scene and look around for clues, evidence."

"Can we get you something?" asked Rizzo to Dickory.

Dickory shook his head.

"I think we should do this at another time," said Billie. "He's obviously upset."

Rizzo looked at her. "We're all upset. But we need to understand what happened."

"Right now?" asked Billie. "Look at him. He can't even talk. We need to give him some room."

"We need to find out what happened. When it's clear in his head." Rizzo paused. "And before he's had too much time… to think about it."

"You think he did it?" Billie's eyes were wide. Her nostrils were twitching wildly. "Look at him. Think about what he's been through. Have you no heart?"

"Have you no brain?" shouted Rizzo.

Dickory started peeping anxiously. Rizzo and Billie looked at him. He was crying. That was a first. Animals don't cry. At least they never had before. To their knowledge.

Rizzo softened his voice. "We need to understand what happened, Dickory. Can you tell us?"

"He's frightened. Let him be," said Billie.

"I couldn't sleep," said Dickory quietly. "I woke up and saw Hickory was gone. Sometimes he goes for long walks. I don't know why. He just does." Dickory rubbed his wet eyes with a tiny hand, then wiped the moistness on his ruffled fur.

"I just walked around for a while. I smelled Hickory in a room. But it smelled bad. I got nervous. But I went in and turned on a light. I saw… you know… you saw it. It was Hickory. Blood all over. I felt faint. I could barely get myself to pull the alarm. It was horrible."

Billie softened her voice. "Did you see anyone. Any idea how this happened? Anyone leaving the room?"

Dickory shook his head and wiped away more tears. "I loved him," he said.

"He's upset. Shocked. He needs rest," said Billie to Rizzo. "He needs rest," she repeated louder and more forcefully.

Julius came back into the room. "I found…"

Rizzo cut him off. "Take Dickory back to his room." Rizzo glanced at Billie but was still talking to Julius. "Keep an eye on him."

"For how long?" asked Julius.

"Until I say so," said Rizzo.

Billie glared at Rizzo.

Julius gently cupped Dickory in his hands and carried him out.

"You're the president, Rizzo, not a dictator."

"And neither are you, Billie. We have rules. You want to change the rules, get the legislators to vote on it."

"That would take days or weeks," said Billie. "We need swift justice. Justice delayed is justice denied."

"Law and order exist for the purpose of establishing justice," quoted Rizzo.

"And when they fail in this purpose, they become the dangerously structured dams that block the flow of social progress," responded Billie.

They stared silently at each other. Then Billie walked out of the room, angry. Justice had not been done, she thought.

With a great flapping sound, Evan flew down from the rafters. He had been watching the entire time. He landed on the table in front of Rizzo, his eyes unblinking, his beak only inches away. "She is battling for justice."

Rizzo was angry at Evan for this intrusion on a private conversation. A private government conversation. But he was also angry at Billie. Looking straight into Evan's black hole eyes, he asked, "Do you even understand what you're saying, or do you just repeat things you've heard?"

Evan yawned wide, showing the cavernous abyss of his mouth. "She is battling." He shut his mouth and brought his face just a bit closer to Rizzo. "For justice." Then he flew off.

Chapter 17

In the darkness, a small lamp lit up Julius's black furry head from above. The light and shadows made his otherwise jovial face seem menacing. He blinked, as the light was harsh in his eyes. Rizzo sat in the dark across from him, a small shadow limned with a bright yellow corona.

"Why the darkness?" asked Julius.

"I just don't want to wake the others," said Rizzo.

"And why the secrecy?" asked Julius.

"I just don't want to alarm anyone," said Rizzo.

Julius blinked, squinted, blinked again. "The light is kind of harsh. It's hard to see you. Or anything."

"Sorry." Rizzo moved the lamp so it shone between them instead of directly on Julius. "Tell me what you found out."

"Hickory was attacked by a larger, carnivorous animal. A predator."

"How can you tell?"

"The teeth marks. Canines. And the footprints in the blood."

"A dog?"

"Maybe. Or a related animal. But not as large as any of our dogs."

"But not another mouse."

"Not a mouse."

"So not Dickory."

"Definitely not Dickory."

"Have you narrowed it down?"

"Just to a small canine."

"So if it's a small canine, but not one of our dogs, then who can it possibly be?"

"That's the puzzle for sure."

"Could you be mistaken?"

"Sure. I don't think so, but… no I don't think so."

"Someone staged it?"

"Seems unlikely. And why?"

"To blame another animal?"

"Then you'd make it look like one of our animals. Not some unknown creature."

"True." Rizzo paused in thought, staring at the ceiling. Julius grew uncomfortable. Finally, Rizzo continued, "As Sherlock Holmes said, 'When you have eliminated the impossible, whatever remains, however improbable, must be the truth.'"

"Never heard of him."

"You should. Look him up."

"OK, I'll do that," said Julius, but he wasn't very much of a reader.

"See you in the morning," said Rizzo as he snapped off the light and wandered back to his bed.

Julius's eyes weren't as good in the dark as Rizzo's, so he felt his way toward the dimly lit hallway, banging his knees and cursing lightly as he stumbled away.

Chapter 18

Animerica could be called prosperous by most measures. The farms were producing enough food for all. The animals each had shelter. Of course, they had shelter when humans ran the lab, but now many had been able to move out of cages and into nice places. Others had chosen to decorate their cages, something that had never occurred to them before Day 1. Of course, a lot had changed since then, but it was hard for them to grasp why these things suddenly mattered—colors, decorations, things of beauty.

Other signs of prosperity included leisure activities: sports and nightclubs and entertainment and simple social gatherings. There was more socializing among the animals, at least a different kind of socializing than previously. This kind of socializing wasn't for protection or for hunting or for mating— at least not directly. There was intraspecies socializing but also, to a limited degree, interspecies socializing, which is something that had rarely been seen before. If ever. And there was gossip. Of course, the animal murders were a major source of gossip. Fear is a boundless generator of gossip.

A rumor began that a human was murdering the animals. It's not clear where this rumor started, though it easily could have started simultaneously from many different sources. It was an easy explanation. And humans had, in the past, easily murdered animals without much thought, so it made some sense. Rizzo had done what he could to integrate humans with animals, but it was difficult. There were lingering bad feelings. Most of these humans, though, were children, and one of his idealistic goals was for Animerica to be a place for all animals; human animals too.

Cagney and Billie also dreamt of an Animerica that included all animals, but they were ambivalent about humans. Were they animals? Were they something else? And could they be forgiven for their past evils? Did they have a memory of those deeds? Did they inherit those behaviors? Or must they be punished for those actions simply as a means of obtaining justice for the cruelties imposed on animals by humans? Some animals believed in a supreme being. Some believed in an afterlife where rewards and punishments were meted out by this supreme being. But Cagney and Billie saw this as silly superstition from small-minded animals. They believed what was testable and provable, not some invisible kings and demons. They believed in fairness and justice.

In that spirit of fairness and justice they saw an opportunity. They hadn't started the rumors about humans murdering animals, but they saw that it advanced their cause. If humans were to be condemned for their past behaviors, to make sure they never ever happen again, then these rumors were an easy way to convince the other animals. Sometimes logic and reason didn't work, especially for those of the lower species. And so using emotions to drive an argument that they already knew philosophically and intellectually was right… well the result was good and fair, which was the most important thing.

Rizzo had been good to the humans. He instituted the education program for them. He openly wanted to include them in society. He was friendly with Charlie and Sheila and Archie. And with Julius, who was almost human himself. They just made sure to point out these connections. To everyone. At every opportunity. They didn't connect the dots—the other animals did that. Billie and Cagney felt good about this. As they should. Doing the right thing always made them feel good.

Chapter 19

Rizzo took one of his regular strolls around the lab. It had been a while since his last stroll, but he'd had a lot of work and now it seemed like many things were progressing without his oversight. Things were going well. He liked walking and observing. He called it management by wandering around, or "MBWA," which he had read somewhere but couldn't remember where. He passed the farms, which had been expanded since Day 1. A good number of animals worked in the farms. No longer sterile white plastic containers of sparse vegetation under harsh heat lamps, the farms were now fields of soil that went on for yards and yards. The plants were not just small individual stalks but rows of corn and wheat and potatoes and small plots for other vegetables. The animals would learn how to get the plants to flourish in the lab's environment before harvesting them on a grand scale.

In the fields, the animals seemed happy. Not always, of course. There was the occasional cursing. Fights broke out now and then. But the animals felt a sense of accomplishment for the first times in their lives. They were working for themselves and in turn for the good of the entire community.

And they were using tools that they had built. Or that others had built and sold to them. The tools made their work easier, so they were happy to pay for them. And some animals were making a very good living designing the tools and selling them. The currency system they had set up was working well. Innovation was increasing, leading to a rising standard of living, leading to greater overall wealth, leading to more innovation. It was the great cycle he'd learned about. And it was happening.

Artwork had started appearing on walls. Since Day 1, the animals had developed senses of identity and individuality. Art helped them express that. Some created their own artwork, but a small group of artists began selling their works to the other animals. Rizzo loved to see new artwork each time he strolled around. He didn't always understand it. Or like it. But it fascinated him to know that these animals wanted to be individuals, wanted to express their unique tastes, and were no longer so interested in conforming. Animal behavior was changing.

They were building habitats, too. Nice ones. Comfortable ones. Not just fancy cages, but intricate structures. Some beautiful. Some bizarre. All unique.

Entertainment businesses had sprung up. Animals had never before known or thought about leisure time, but now they had free time and had desires besides eating and procreating. Not that those weren't still high on the list as demonstrated by the restaurants, bars, nightclubs, and discotheques that had also been opening in what became known as the Entertainment District.

The Inspiration Project was an amazing success. When he walked by that area of the lab, it still looked like a lab. But this one had animals scampering around it, turning knobs, peering through microscopes, pressing buttons, taking notes. Some really great work had come out of this project. Startup companies got funded, created new inventions, and grew wildly successful. Investors took risks and some of them did very well. The inventions were turned into products that made life easier for everyone. And the patent system that the government created made sure that inventors had protection from theft of their creations and that all animals, wealthy or not, competed equally in the free market.

And the population was growing, which was also a good sign. Better yet, it was growing slowly, not rampantly. That meant that society could manage the resources for everyone.

And humans were making progress, too. The children that had showed up were being taught to fit into the new society. That part was admittedly difficult. There were lingering bad feelings among the animals. The human children worked in the fields performing manual labor, which was very easy for them given their size compared to most of the animals. When not working in the fields, or studying in school, they stayed mostly to themselves. The few human adults who had shown up took care of the children when not doing their jobs in the lab.

Not everything was perfect, of course. Rizzo had not expected perfection, so it didn't surprise him that there were fights, theft, vandalism, and other mostly minor crimes.

There were still the murders, though. Once in a while an animal would be found badly mauled and eaten. The animals in Animerica were not saints, but they had it good enough that serious crimes were rare. They had enough food that there was no need to eat each other. And since Day 1, for whatever reason, their more vicious instincts had been dulled if not eliminated altogether for most of the animals. So it puzzled Rizzo that these murders were still occurring and that none of the others had come forward as witnesses. Julius had been working with some of the lab rats to design a better security system throughout the lab that might be able to catch the criminal in the act, so there was hope that this killing spree would end soon.

Chapter 20

About a week after Hickory was found murdered, another mouse was found in a different part of the lab. In a remote section. Again, what was found was a lump of chewed flesh in a pool of splattered blood. It took a while to identify it. The mouse had been a loner, given to wandering off by itself. To contemplate the world. It didn't have many friends, so no one knew how long ago it had been killed.

Dickory had been under watch and while he was still under suspicion in Hickory's murder, most animals believed him to be innocent.

Julius looked into this second murder and decided that it was the same killer. The same marks, the same pattern. Still it didn't fit the description of any of the animals in the lab. Although there were now hundreds of animals in the labs, Julius checked on each and every one of them and began keeping track of them. Keeping notes on some of them.

Julius looked into the stories of Sherlock Homes, at Rizzo's suggestion. He started studying real detectives, too. And forensics. He even had Carrie Lee make him a deerstalker cap that he alternated with his security cap.

A few weeks after that, another corpse was found. A rabbit. Again in a remote part of the lab. Again with the same marks, same pattern.

All of the animals were getting noticeably anxious. Nervous. Scared—just a little. While previously they had all been happy—after all Animerica was turning out to be a much better place than any of them had experienced before—but now there was suspicion. They didn't all trust each other completely. It started slowly, but a keen observer could see the changes. After a while, the changes were obvious to everyone.

The society started to develop cliques. Cats hung out mostly with other cats. Dogs kept in touch mostly with other dogs. Birds with birds. Rodents socialized mostly with rodents, and among rodents, rats with rats, mice with mice, and Guinea pigs with Guinea pigs.

Among the rodents, the discussion often centered on whether the cats had been killing the rodents. The cats seemed rather lazy, but despite the fact that the farms produced enough food for all, they did have that killer instinct.

The cats were resentful of these furtive implications and accusations. They believed it must be the birds. And perhaps the birds were spreading rumors about the cats to deflect the suspicion. Then again, it could have been the dogs, though the dogs didn't seem smart enough. And yet, all of the animals had become smarter since Day 1. Who knew how clever the dogs might have become? Clever enough to hide their cunning, perhaps.

Rizzo saw the changes occurring. He met often with Julius, but Julius had no clues. He was perplexed. He had really been thorough in his examinations, but he was new at this and doubted his abilities. Yet, he spent most of his free time poring over pictures, interviewing other animals, drawing diagrams, and writing up motives and scenarios. He had the dogs try to track the perpetrators, but for some reason they weren't able to connect the scent with any of the animals in Animerica. The various chemicals and cleaners in the lab were overpowering and may have made it difficult to identify individual odors. Or maybe as their intelligence had suddenly increased, their olfactory abilities had declined. After all, human senses were fairly poor even though their intelligence levels had been very high. Is there some kind of balance, some conservation principle? Maybe an intelligent brain can only handle so much information, so the greater amount of processing devoted to high-level thought, the less was available for interpreting sensory input.

Or maybe the dogs were just lying to him.

And of course all of the animals suspected the humans.

Chapter 21

Cagney called out to Rizzo. "We'd like to talk to you."

It had been a long night and Rizzo was tired. The murders had been occupying his thoughts. He had been thinking about putting up a door to his room. He had never thought about privacy before. Certainly not before Day 1. But he'd been thinking about it more and more these days. That is Rule Number 6 of The Seven Rights and Responsibilities after all.

"Give me a minute," he called out. He stumbled to the toilet, yawned, relieved himself, strolled to the wash basin and washed his face. Then he came around from behind the curtain of his sleeping area.

Cagney nodded to Rizzo. Billie was behind him. This seemed to be a common positioning whenever they approached him about some matter, which was often these days. At least more often than he liked.

"We'd like to talk to you about an idea we have," said Billie. She looked at Cagney. Cagney looked at Rizzo. Rizzo looked skyward, then caught himself and looked directly at Cagney. That intimidated Cagney, but he got intimidated easily.

"Shoot," said Rizzo.

Cagney turned to look at Billie.

"It's about fairness," said Billie to Cagney.

"Yes," said Cagney, turning back to Rizzo. "It's about fairness."

"OK," said Rizzo. "Fairness is important." This seemed to be their buzzword. Everything they did, Cagney and Billie, related to fairness.

"Fairness is most important," shot back Billie. "It's not just important... it's everything."

Rizzo continued looking at Cagney. "So what's this idea?"

"It's not just an idea," said Billie. "It's a concept. A plan. A philosophy for our whole society."

"Uh… yes," said Cagney. "Different animals have different needs."

"Go on," said Rizzo.

Cagney looked back at Billie who nodded to him. "They have different needs and different capabilities. The government must require equality. It must require that all animals are treated equally. Fairly."

"I think they are," said Rizzo. "Are you aware that they're not?"

"Of course not," said Billie angrily. "We must eliminate speciesism."

Rizzo squinted at them. Somewhere he'd heard of this but had not been paying attention. He had work to get done. That was his personal mantra. He could figure out what they were talking about, but he wanted to hear it from them. "What's that?"

"It's a form of discrimination, an oppressive belief system. It's the differing treatment of individuals based on their species."

"It's freaking wrong," shouted Billie.

"But we are all different," said Rizzo. He generally liked to stay calm, but it had the added benefit of really pissing off Billie when she was worked up.

Cagney saw Billie losing control of the discussion, so he jumped in before she could. "We want to encourage animals to report incidents of species discrimination. You must admit that lately animals have been associating mostly with their own species. It's a dangerous kind of discrimination."

"You mean they shouldn't be able to choose with whom they want to associate?"

"No, of course not. But you must see how different animals stick together and avoid others. It's hurting our concept of one place for all animals. Our concept of Animerica."

"OK, what do you suggest?"

"That we look into ways of eliminating discrimination."

"OK," said Rizzo. "And how, exactly, do we define discrimination?"

"We know it when we see it, Rizzo," said Billie.

Cagney stepped back and nuzzled her to calm her. It seemed to do the opposite. "When an animal can show that they are being discriminated against solely based on their species, they should be allowed to petition the government to correct it."

"But we all have different capabilities, Cagney," responded Rizzo. "Some are big, some are small. Some have opposable thumbs, some have tails. Some tails are prehensile while others are... cosmetic."

"So they petition the government. The government decides. If it's not a valid complaint, it's dismissed. No harm, no foul." He looked at Billie, smiled, and spelled it: "F-O-U-L." She didn't smile back.

"Well, you're in charge of the legislature. If you can get it passed, I'll take a look at it. Seems unnecessary, maybe even counterproductive, but... you get it passed and I'll take a look at it."

"Great," said Cagney. "Thanks, Rizzo." He turned to go.

"That includes humans," said Billie with a laser stare at Rizzo.

"You mean that they'd be covered by this new law? They could report discrimination, right. That makes sense."

"No. I mean that animals can report when humans are given preference over them. We live in an animal world. One that broke free from the oppression of humans. We need to make sure that we don't devolve into that world from which we escaped."

"It seems to me," said Rizzo, "that humans helped us break free somehow. In this lab. Before they disappeared."

"So you give the enslavers a pass because some of them were nice task masters. You think they helped us because they wanted to help animals or because they were looking to advance their own race? We were just a side effect."

"The ones who are here now weren't the ones who 'enslaved us'," Rizzo responded, wishing he had hands and fingers that allowed air quotes. "If we're to be an equal society, it needs to be equal for all."

"And it will be," said Billie. "And it will make up for past injustices." She turned and left. She needed to get in the last word—that's the way she was. As if the last word meant she had "won" the argument.

Chapter 22

Julius lounged in a brightly colored folding chair on the beach of a tropical jungle. At his side was a beautiful female ape in a matching chair. They discussed security and politics, eating bananas under the shade of a palm tree whose leaves swayed in the slight, cool breeze. He reached over and grasped his cocktail glass and brought it up to his face, which led him into a short soliloquy about the advantages of an opposable thumb. The tiny umbrella, no longer weighted down by the now melted ice, fell into the fine white sand. With his other hand, he snapped his fingers, which led to yet another short soliloquy about opposable thumbs. The female was enthralled, watching him, sipping from her glass, and nodding very slightly from time to time.

A human waiter, dressed formally in black and white, approached the two of them, one hand balancing a plate of glasses with a cloth draped over his angled arm. His black shoes caused little eruptions of sand with each step. It seemed he had heard Julius' fingers snap from yards away, maybe miles away, but he made steady progress, unslowed by the soft sand. When he reached the two apes, he bent lower and in a subservient British accent said, "Bwap, bwap, bwap!"

The sound of the Animal Lab alarm system seeped slowly into Julius' brain but when it did, he awoke immediately. The adrenalin that erupted throughout his body jerked him awake. The sudden transformation from sluggish dream state to hyper-focused action was a jarring one, but one that Julius had taught himself to master. And take pride in.

He swiveled from his bed, considered not throwing on pants but decided that the time debating the decision would take longer than doing it, so he grabbed the pair by his bed and jumped into them, two feet at one time. Yes, Julius had started wearing clothing, as had many of the animals in the lab. It seemed uncivilized… or embarrassing now not to do so.

Julius slammed open the door from his room into the hallway. It was dusk, and the hall lights were dim, but a small trail of red LEDs on the floor blinked a sequence showing the direction of the disturbance. He ran in the direction they pointed. At some places where the lighting was poor or trash cans were left in the hallways for pickup the next day, he grabbed the overhead bars he'd had installed to swing through the hallways. It was also convenient as animals began sleepily coming out of their rooms to find out what was going on, creating sudden obstacles on the ground. The ability to both run and swing made him well-equipped to do his job, and of course the thought of his opposable thumbs entered his thoughts, but just briefly. His overriding thoughts were about what or who had set off the alarm.

The lights directed him to a far-off room in the lab. Swinging around a corner, he could hear something. Movement. Growling. Animal-like—a noise like he hadn't heard since before Day 1, something he only now realized that he hadn't heard since then. He could also sense something. Smelled an odor of fear. Felt a heat like anger.

Julius swung into the doorway and froze. The room was dark, but he felt a presence. Pacing. He wasn't so much frightened as he was surprised. The sense in the room was... primitive. His eyes were having trouble adjusting. He blinked a few times, heard something pacing back and forth. It was small, but softly growling. Julius reach along the wall to find the light switch. He rubbed all over where it should have been, but found nothing. Two glowing eyes appeared. Unblinking. He knew it could see him, but he couldn't make out more than an outline. He frantically swiped his palm all over the wall where he thought the light should be. Julius wasn't afraid of much, but darkness put him at a big disadvantage. Crazy conspiratorial thoughts came into his head about someone removing the light switch until his palm caught the corner of it.

Julius smacked the switch and the white light filled the room. An animal—a very young predatory animal—ran into a corner but swiveled around quickly to glare at him. Its fur was dirty and ruffled. It was lean and haggard. Its eyes were black with circles around them. Patches of fur were falling out. Or growing in—Julius couldn't be sure. It looked like a small dog. But different.

A young mouse, shivering with fright, ran from under a desk in the room to the door beside Julius. "He's vicious!" screamed the mouse. "He tried to catch me! He tried to eat me! He's not one of us!"

"You okay?" asked Julius.

"I guess," said the mouse, shivering uncontrollably.

"You get to the infirmary. Get checked out. I'll need to talk to you later."

The mouse backed out, keeping its eyes on the predator. A crowd had started to gather outside the door, but kept its distance. One of the other mice accompanied this one down the hallway.

Rizzo ran to the doorway, out of breath.

Julius glanced down at Rizzo then back up at the animal. "What is it?"

"A coyote," replied Rizzo.

At this point Billie came running into the doorway, Cagney right behind her. Rizzo nodded at them.

"Never heard of such a thing," said Julius. "Looks like a mangy dog."

"It's related," said Rizzo. "But there weren't any in the lab. They weren't domesticated. Or used in research. They're scavengers. The question is, where did this one come from? And how did it get into the lab?"

"The question is," said Billie, "what do we do with this one?"

"I think the immediate answer is obvious," said Rizzo. "Julius, do you think you can pick it up?"

"Will it bite?"

"Maybe. Can you search the drawers in here? There might be gloves in the drawers."

"I'll look." Slowly, keeping his eyes on the coyote, Julius tiptoed over to the drawers, opening them and peering inside. The coyote stood frozen in a corner, watching him, unblinking.

"Then what?" asked Billie.

"Then," Rizzo replied, "we put it in a cage until…"

"No!" shouted Billie.

The coyote lunged toward the door. Julius pivoted and grabbed the coyote with one hand as it got close to Billie, Cagney, and Rizzo. The animal howled and sunk its teeth into Julius' arm. Julius let out his own howl, then pried the animal's jaws off his arm with his other hand. The coyote twisted and turned to get free, but Julius held him tight. The guttural sounds coming from the coyote echoed throughout the room and into the hallway as all the other animals moved back and away from the commotion.

"You OK?" asked Rizzo.

"I've got him," said Julius.

"Take him to Lab Room 106. There are a number of unused cages there."

"No," insisted Billie. "We don't put animals in cages. Humans did that. We don't do it to our own."

"Then what would you suggest?" asked Rizzo.

"We just don't put animals in cages. It's wrong. It's unanimal."

Rizzo looked at her for a moment with obvious frustration. Her demands and proposals were getting to be problematic. While he once found them annoying, he now found them to be ridiculous. Frivolous. Impediments to the great progress they'd been making. He looked back at Julius and the violently squirming young coyote in his hands. "Until Billie thinks of a better way to protect us from him and him from some of us, put him in a cage and arrange for food and water. And get to the infirmary to have your arm looked at."

"Will do," said Julius as he carried the writhing animal out into the hallway.

"And thanks, Julius," said Rizzo. "Good work. Really good work."

Julius shrugged. With Julius already turned to go, Rizzo couldn't see the smile on Julius' face.

"Cruel," said Billie to Rizzo.

"I'm going back to bed," said Rizzo. "We can hold a meeting in the morning." He turned to go. As he walked out, he heard a distinctly primitive hiss behind his back.

Chapter 23

Billie sat outside the cage, staring at the young, wild coyote pacing back and forth nervously. It mostly ignored her, ignored all its surroundings. It just perpetually paced, except when a plate of food was brought in twice a day. Then it would back into a corner, stare and growl at the animal that brought it in. When the animal left, it would stare and growl at the plate for a while. Then it would cautiously approach it, circle it while sniffing vigorously. Without warning, it would attack the food like prey and claw it back to the far corner of the cage, eating it while staring straight ahead, on the lookout for attackers.

Billie would watch the coyote with fascination. It wasn't more than a few years old, she guessed. It was so primitive. She found that interesting. Exciting? It worked on instinct. It reminded her of how she used to be. How all of them used to be.

She had been coming to the cage every day for weeks. She would talk to the coyote about philosophy and politics. It didn't understand, she knew. It was primitive. Pure. Billie could refine her ideas here without the distraction of constantly explaining them, like she did with Cagney, or defending them, like she did with Rizzo.

"You shouldn't be in a cage. That's what humans did to us. We should not be doing it to each other. We need to rise above that behavior. We need to be better than humans."

The coyote paced.

"Did you know they kept us in cages here? In this laboratory. They experimented on us to find cures for their diseases. Not cures for us. For them. Many of us died from these experiments. Some just died from neglect. It didn't matter to them. We didn't matter to them."

The coyote paced.

"Something happened on Day 1. Something changed us. At least it changed us in the lab. We acquired complex thought. Most importantly, we discovered the ability to distinguish between good and evil. Maybe that was our greatest accomplishment. Distinguishing between good and evil."

The coyote paced.

"You're no different than us. You're just not where we are. Yet. You deserve justice. You deserve freedom. You deserve fairness."

The coyote paced.

"You're not the enemy. You shouldn't be in a cage. This isn't fair. If anyone should be in a cage, if any species should be in a cage, it's the humans. After what they did to us. They already knew right from wrong. And they did it anyway."

The coyote paced.

"There's a problem in our seeming prosperity. Our society has a veneer of material wealth while hiding the decaying interior. Spiritual perfection is more important than just having stuff. Or making stuff. If we put on fancy clothes and live in fine enclosures and have time for leisure, is that the answer to why we've developed our superior intelligence? Or should we seek a higher purpose of rooting out injustice and prejudice and creating a truly equal society for all animals, for all species? I say the latter. Otherwise, why? What is our purpose?

"So we have a problem. Our problem is that animals have been obedient, and don't know anything but obedience. Originally to humans, and now to a system of stifling, unjust, and unfair rules that we've created to replace the human rules. The human rules were for their benefit not ours. They were incomprehensible to us. But we obeyed. Now we have our own rules, but these rules simply replace the human rules. They do nothing to bring about justice and fairness, which are on a higher plane of abstraction. No rules can really encompass them. It's about treating each animal equally. Having each succeed at their goals equally. Each animal having as much as any other animal.

"And yet look at you in this cage. This cage represents the worst of our new society. The humanity of our new society. Our problem is that animals have obeyed the dictates of humans for centuries and now the dictates of other animals… and millions have died and been killed because of this obedience. Our problem is that animals are obedient all throughout the lab. Our problem is that our so-called prosperity hides the injustices in Animerica. Our problem is that animals are obedient and so we have put an innocent, pure animal in a cage for doing what wild animals do. I'm beginning to believe that the wrong animals are running the country. That's our problem. And I'm sad to say that I'm part of the problem. That must change if our society is to change."

The coyote stopped pacing. It turned and stared at her. Did it understand her, she wondered? Some truths, she thought, really are self-evident. She felt good, confident, as she walked out of the lab into the hallway.

The coyote heard, or sensed a slight movement near the ceiling, and jerked its head up in that direction at a small, black mass. Evan shook out his wings. "Be the change that you wish to see in the world," he said. The coyote licked its lips. "Beware the change that you wish to see in the world," said Evan then flew away.

Chapter 24

The legislature sat around the table in Independence Room, with Billie at the head, Cagney to one side, and Rizzo to the other. The animals of the legislature were an eclectic combination around the table, all shapes, sizes, and colors, heads bobbing, mouths moving, quietly discussing, debating, disagreeing while waiting for the session to come to order. From the rafters, Evan watched quietly, sporadically pausing to preen.

"The meeting will come to order," said Billie, banging her tiny gavel, which hardly made more than a quiet tink. The murmuring continued. "Come to order, come to order," shouted Billie, but the murmuring continued. The tink of her gavel didn't even reach the ears of Cagney and Rizzo beside her. Rizzo motioned to Julius, sitting in one of the observer chairs by the door. Julius stood, clapped his hands several times and said, "Quiet!"

Every animal stopped immediately and turned toward Julius. He sat down. From the front, they heard, "The meeting will come to order" from Rizzo.

Billie glared at Rizzo who just smiled at her and nodded. Billie cleared her throat.

"Today we will be taking a great step in our new society. A step toward equality. Something the humans tried and failed. Something animals have never tried. But we can learn from the failures of humans. They put in place slogans, but no real policies. And when they did create policies, they did not enforce them. And when they enforced them, they did not enforce them with vigor. With courage. With... teeth!

"But we animals will do that. This policy that we are about to vote on is the result of much thought. So much thought. I know that I have spent much of my time thinking about policies that will benefit not just one of us but all of us. And I don't mean just those on the inside of this lab. I mean all animals everywhere. Are we due special benefits because of our location? Are we due special treatment because we were placed in this laboratory and had the benefits brought about on Day 1 while others, through no fault of their own, did not?

"If we are going to create the Great Society—which we must—then it must include all animals and treat all animals equally. Give all animals opportunities. If you see an animal that is destitute, that is impoverished, that is unempowered, that is disenfranchised…" She paused for effect. Nearly every eye was on her. Except Arnold, whose eyes were staring at the floor. He was listening. Thinking. His eyesight wasn't very good anyway, so there was little point in staring at Billie. Better not to be distracted, he thought, but rather to listen to the words. And consider them.

"If an animal is lacking resources, lacking empowerment, that means that some animal, some circumstance… or some human… has singled out that creature and denied it its rights. We know what it's like to access the privilege of a particular location, but now we know what it is like to be born into one that could have destined us to something else. We have seen it firsthand with the young, native coyote that miraculously appeared here."

"This bill that we are about to sign, makes all animals welcome here. Regardless of where they were born. Regardless of how they got here." She looked around the room. A smattering of applause started that grew louder as most of the legislators joined in. "This is justice! This is fairness!" The applause grew louder, and she smiled. "This is Animerica!"

Billie looked around. She nodded to the crowd, which continued clapping. She sat down slowly, dramatically, surveying the room, nodding to the crowd, pointing at a few individuals, beaming. She let the applause continue for some time. When it started to get quieter, she said, "Now let us take the vote." This time she was pleased that the crowd couldn't hear her, but eventually the applause died out. "Now let us take the vote," she repeated.

"Billie," said Rizzo. "I'd like to say a few words first." He had a way of talking quietly but drawing everyone's attention.

Billie had difficulty hiding her anger. Rizzo was about to take credit. He wanted to have the last word. To take the attention, and the recognition, away from her. She nodded at him, knowing that her voice would squeak if she said anything. As he stood, her mind raced with ways to recapture the credit she deserved once he gave his speech.

"This is a good thing we're doing today," said Rizzo. "Animerica must be a welcoming place to all." There was a smattering of applause. "And I commend Cagney for his devotion to leading the effort on this bill." He paused and nodded at Cagney who smiled back sheepishly. "And of course to Billie." He nodded to Billie who was too deep in thought about recapturing the credit to hear or acknowledge Rizzo's words.

"Fairness and justice are great ideals," Rizzo continued, "but they must be enacted through law and order. Security is also a great ideal. Animerica is a new society. We are trying to make it successful, and so far, we have prospered." There was more applause. Rizzo continued, "But we can only continue to prosper... in fact, we can only continue to survive... if we take things slowly. We must act with caution. We don't know what happened on Day 1. We don't know why we are the way we are. And more importantly, we don't know much about the world outside the laboratory.

"That's why I have proposed the amendments to the bill that are written on the papers being distributed to you now."

Julius had gotten up when Rizzo started speaking and began handing out papers to the legislators. Billie would have been angry if she had noticed. If she had not been so lost in thought. But she saw it now and was fuming. She should have been told about this beforehand. Rizzo had no right to spring something like this without warning. She had crafted a perfect bill and there was no need for amendments. Rizzo had gone behind her tail.

"The amendments propose a guard unit to be posted around the periphery to find out where the wild animals are getting in."

"Naturals!" shouted Billie, rising up on her hind legs. Rizzo looked at her puzzled. "Do not call them 'wild'!" she shouted. "They are 'naturals.' We cannot denigrate them like the humans did. They are our brothers and sisters. In fact, they are more pure than us because we evolved from them. We must respect them. Help them. Not disparage them!"

Rizzo paused in thought. He didn't want an argument. Not now. That wouldn't help his effort. "Yes, we must help them," he said. "We must help them learn our language, learn some basic skills, understand the rules of

Animerica. We must help them make an orderly entrance to our new society."

"And while they are learning all this, what do you propose to do with them?" asked Billie.

"It's in the amendment," replied Rizzo to the legislators, not to Billie. "We keep them in segregation."

"So now we segregate animals. Are we no better than humans?"

"We keep them apart until we assess the risks. Until we understand the situation. Until they learn and accept our very new way of life."

"And this is what you call justice? This is what you call fairness?"

"And if you look at the last few pages of the handout," said Rizzo, ignoring Billie, "you'll see the images... and I apologize for this... you'll see the images of those animals that were found dead from a wild animal that we still don't understand. I need not remind you that fairness applies not just to those on the outside, but to those inside the laboratory. We were elected to protect those inside the laboratory."

Rizzo sat down as the legislators viewed the gruesome pictures. Some said nothing. Some groaned at each picture. Some looked away. Some pages were blotted with tears.

A vote was taken, and Billie's bill passed. Rizzo's amendment passed too.

Chapter 25

Things were good in Animerica. Food production had been increasing, and there was plenty of space to expand. And with more prosperity, and more leisure activities available, the population had grown consistently but not wildly like would have happened in the wild. A nice sign of progress. And prosperity.

At first, the issue of wild animals, or "naturals," had been a mostly hypothetical one. Other than the one coyote, there had been no others. Speculation grew that the coyote had not actually been from outside the lab. That it had been brought there by humans for some experiment that never got under way. Or maybe the result of an experiment gone bad. Or smuggled in by one of the human children that still showed up from time to time.

Then some of the animals started noticing others that looked different. For example, most of the animals in the lab had taken to wearing clothes. At least some minimal clothes. There was suddenly a feeling of modesty, and shame, that they had never experienced before. At least not before Day 1. But some animals still didn't wear any clothes. No one said anything. At least not to their faces.

Some animals talked very little. Since speech was a very new thing, most animals were delighted to use it. Constantly. Many too much.

Of course, not talking was not a clear indication of something wrong. Arnold, for example, talked very little and usually only to answer a question. And even then, he conserved his words.

Then things started to go missing. Small things usually, but also food, which didn't make sense because there was plenty for everyone.

There were other strange things, too. Defecation in corners. Under tables. Something that they gave no thought before Day 1 now seemed disgusting. Uncivilized. And why would any animal do that when there was a fully functioning plumbing system including toilets that were accessible for all?

And then some murders again. Small animals found eaten or partially eaten. The coyote was still in a cage, so that eliminated one suspect. The rumors and theories went wild.

And then the new species appeared. And it was clear that somewhere, somehow, wild animals were getting in. And so the Great Animal Debates began.

The proposed solutions ran the gamut, though some objected to the term "solution" because there was not a problem to be solved but an issue to be resolved.

Those at one extreme of the debate, calling themselves the Preservers, said the wild animals should be kept out entirely. That a border patrol needed to be established to patrol the lab perimeters, track incoming animals to find out where they were getting in, force them back out, and seal the opening. The ones who are here should be rounded up and exiled. Animerica is a civilized society. We can't risk more murders, they said. And we can't clean up feces. And we can't house them and provide services for them. We have a good life that we built, and we shouldn't let outsiders destroy it.

Those at the other extreme of the debate, calling themselves the Reformers, said that the naturals must be welcomed. The citizens of Animerica had no right to keep others out. Why should one's physical location on Day 1 arbitrarily dictate a privilege that those in other locations didn't get? And why should humans decide which animals get which rights. After all, it was humans that decided which animals were brought to the lab—without their permission—and which ones were not. Are animals still subservient to humans?

And besides, the Reformers said, the naturals were strong. Lab animals had lived in cages for so long that they no longer had their natural strength and endurance. And since the founding of Animerica, the animals had gotten softer. Things were easier. Why not bring in naturals to do the labor that Animericans no longer wanted to do.

Preservers scoffed at this. Why assume that Animericans couldn't perform physical labor. While their intelligence had increased overall, it wasn't uniform. Not all animals could perform complex tasks. And some just liked physical labor. Some were built for it.

The Reformers were horrified by such arguments. Saying that some animals were built for labor is repugnant. It's prejudice. It's speciesism.

Are you blind, responded the Preservers? Do you actually think that a mouse can do the same labor as a monkey?

Are you stupid, responded the Reformers? The point is that you can't classify an animal according to its species. Some mice are strong. Some monkeys are weak.

"But all wilds are strong?" asked the Preservers.

"Of course," responded the Reformers, "all naturals are strong."

"And you're willing to risk the safety of the community?" asked the Preservers.

"And you're willing to leave our fellow animals out in the wilderness?" asked the Reformers.

These arguments went on all over the lab, at all times of day. They got heated. Sometimes fights broke out. Although only a few animals actually thought much about the issue, most animals found themselves agreeing with one side or the other. They segregated themselves according to their beliefs.

Rizzo saw this as a serious problem. Billie saw this as a great opportunity.

Billie and Cagney brought up the issue at the legislature again, to make changes to the law they had passed on the issue. She gave grand speeches and made emotional pleas, but most of the animals felt that the matter had been solved. Billie's frustration grew. She knew that sometimes, on issues of morality, an animal had to do the right thing even when others didn't recognize it. Any animal more right than its neighbors constitutes a majority of one. She was determined to be that majority.

Billie and Cagney set up a group to secretly seek out naturals. Aid them. Help them fit into society. Protect them—though they were physically strong, they needed protection from the law that Billie had helped produce but that Rizzo had corrupted into something wrong. Something immoral. Evil. She called this group the Fairness for Every Animal and Reformer. She knew what the acronym spelled, and she liked that. She wanted to eventually eliminate FEAR, and fear would only be eliminated once all animals were treated fairly and equally.

Rizzo decided on a different solution. He set up a border patrol. Animals would walk the corridors, check in corners, try to sniff out any intruders from outside the lab, try to find the pathways into the lab and patch them. Animals were given IDs. To get an ID, each one needed to recite the Seven Rights and Responsibilities. It was a convenient way to determine which animals were from Animerica and which were from the wilderness without. The wild animals didn't know the Seven Rights and Responsibilities, and couldn't read them.

When a wild was found, it was separated from society. Just as Rizzo had set up schools for the human children, he set up schools for the wilds. He wasn't sure if they could be taught, but it seemed like a worthwhile effort. If these wilds could learn basic skills like how to dress, how to use a toilet, and most importantly to override the urge to kill its food, then they could be integrated into society. He didn't know how long it would take, but they had time.

And most importantly, murderers, wild or Animerica citizens, needed to be separated from society. There were calls to put the coyote to death for its multiple murders. Maybe that made sense. Maybe it didn't. Society as a whole needed to debate it. Putting an animal to death shouldn't be done easily or without sentiment. Many called for retribution. Some called for torture. But Rizzo knew that if society required that criminals be killed, it had nothing to do with punishment. The coyote did what it did because that's the way its brain was wired. Putting it to death would not be punishment, but would be required for the safety of the community. Of society. If Animerica decided that death was the right consequence of a crime, it must never be done for "closure" or as "punishment" or as "revenge." Killing an animal did not reverse the crime it had committed. Killing an animal for a crime, was simply to make sure that a threat to others was removed. If that's what Animerica decided. If its evolving legal system called for it.

Chapter 26

Over the next months, Billie started approaching different groups of animals. It started out as casual conversations when Billie "happened to drop by" at various lunch breaks. As animals had been increasingly self-segregating, she could pick out a table for rabbits or dogs, for example, or birds, monkeys, or fellow rats with whom she felt most comfortable.

She started out just giving thoughts off the top of her head, but increasingly they became better rehearsed as she knew the material by heart and saw which arguments resonated best with which groups.

The arguments centered on fairness and justice and one of a few very specific themes. To most animals, she argued that prejudice and discrimination must end. She often threw out a few examples. For example, to the smaller animals she started with stories of being overlooked or passed over by larger animals. After all, the larger animals were simply more visible because of their size. That certainly wasn't fair. To the larger animals, she often talked about assumptions that they weren't as bright as the smaller animals even though some of them were very bright. Or to many animals, she talked about the apes who were perceived as large and smart and so they got a disproportionate share of attention and advantages.

And of course she talked about the humans who had many advantages, especially since they had built the lab to accommodate themselves. They could easily get around. They could reach things high up and low down. Switches, drawers, cabinets were all at levels that they could access easily. And they had been educated for years, especially the older ones, so while animals have roughly the same intelligence and mental abilities, the humans had been exercising those skills for much longer than any of the animals. The humans were a threat to all of the animals, especially given their historical behaviors. Before Day 1.

To her fellow rats, the conversation was a little different. With them, she talked about how they could help the other animals. They had a duty to protect the others from harm. Not physical harm, of course. The rats were physically small. Fierce, but small. But the rats had a better grasp on fairness than the other animals, many of whom seemed to simply want to go to work, come home to their friends and families, relax in their free time, and ignore the injustices around them.

She also asked the animals to relate particular stories of discrimination. She found that animals were swayed more by personal stories—emotional stories—than philosophical abstractions or political ideologies. She encouraged them to talk about incidents when they had been overlooked, treated unfairly, bullied, disenfranchised, or unempowered. Often, they were reticent about talking, but with her encouragement, they came through. She encouraged them to talk about any incidents. It was important to bring these things out into the open. Society could not fix itself, she liked to say, if it didn't recognize where it was broken.

So the animals related their stories, often unaware of the bigotry against them until Billie pointed it out to them. She was doing a very good thing. Opening society's wounds to prepare for the healing. As she continued talking with animals, she started setting up meetings in the conference rooms. That way, she could get larger groups together. And she always invited only one species at a time. That way, they could share their grievances against the other species without fear of retaliation.

Presidential elections were coming up soon, and Billie had not missed that fact. That very important fact.

Chapter 27

"So how's it going?" Rizzo looked around the lab. Animals were busy everywhere, moving things, pressing knobs, peering into lenses, plugging in equipment, typing on keyboards, unplugging equipment. It looked good. It looked like progress.

"Going well," said the monkey in the orange hardhat and holding an electronic clipboard. "We're learning the equipment. Figuring things out."

Rizzo took a deep slow breath of pride and let it out slowly. "Everything according to plan, so far?"

"Pretty much," said the monkey. "Pretty much."

"Anything you need from the government?"

"Nope. Nothing more, thank you."

The monkey was unusually untalkative. Monkeys generally liked to talk about anything. Or nothing. Often nonstop. There were jokes about this. But this monkey was unusually quiet.

"OK," said Rizzo. "I'm glad to hear everything's going well. That you're making progress. You know that I'm from the government, and I'm here to help."

"OK," said the monkey, tapping his stylus on the electronic clipboard.

There was an uncomfortable silence. Rizzo expected the monkey to say something, but he kept standing there tapping. He was looking over in the corner. Rizzo followed his glance. In the corner was a gorilla and a dog eating sandwiches from a bag, talking to each other.

"Nice to see everyone getting along, right?" asked Rizzo.

"Yeah," replied the monkey noncommittally. "Yeah," he repeated.

At that moment, Rizzo heard a loud squeaking coming from the opposite side of the lab. Rizzo turned to see in the far corner, a large clump of mice pushing a small refrigerator. They were climbing on top of each other, shouting orders to each other to coordinate, their feet slipping and sliding on the tile floor, and basically making no progress.

"Well that doesn't seem to be working," said Rizzo, puzzled.

"Yeah. Tell me about it," sighed the monkey.

"Look, I don't mean to tell you how to do your job," said Rizzo, "but what the heck are you doing? Why aren't the dog or the ape, or both, pushing that thing? The mice can't do it."

The monkey came closer, his voice lower. "I'm probably saying this to the wrong person," he confided. "My plan was for the mice and smaller animals to dig conduits and run wires. The gorillas, dogs, and larger animals to move equipment. The monkeys were going to do the programming. They can use the keyboards easily. I had it all planned out and it was working great. We were making progress, maybe even beating our schedules."

"And?" ask Rizzo, though somewhere in the back of his mind, he knew the answer. The general answer. Just not the details.

"One of the animals complained."

"Who?"

"I don't know. Anonymously."

"Complained about what?"

"That I'd been favoring the monkeys to do the 'easy' work. The deskwork. I was just trying to give each animal the job they're best suited to. Things were running smoothly until then.

"Someone from the government came around. Talked about the Fairness for Every Animal and Reformer law. You know. The FEAR law. Told me I had to distribute the jobs evenly. Or rotate. Or something to make things fair. Equal. We have days, like today, when nearly nothing gets done."

"I didn't realize it had gotten this bad."

"You should. You're the president. And you helped pass this law. I'm afraid to even mention it to you. But I had to say something. I can't meet my deadlines and also uphold this law. I just can't do it."

"What can I do?"

"Change the law. No one is happy. You see those mice? They're not happy. They spend an entire day shouting and pushing and get nowhere. You think that's fulfilling? And the ape and the dog. I don't know, maybe they're happy kibitzing all day, but they don't accomplish anything. No one seems happy to me. And fights break out between the species. I have to hire security now. Never had to do that before. It's depressing."

Rizzo sniffed a few times, his whiskers writhing. He had felt so good for a long time. He'd had a sense of accomplishment. He thought things were going so well. That they were building this great new society. And they were. When did things start going wrong? And why hadn't he noticed?

"Presidential elections are coming up," said Rizzo.

"I know," said the monkey, "that's the only reason I brought it up. You know that Cagney is planning on running, right?"

"Cagney? I thought maybe Billie, but…"

"I heard Cagney, but what's the difference. They're the same person. The same bad ideas. I think you're the right person to stop all this."

"Look, I disagree with Billie and Cagney, but they're not bad people. They have good intentions. They're concerned with fairness and justice. So am I."

"It's not the same. It's… just not the same."

At that moment, some shrill whistles were blowing, and Rizzo turned to see a fight breaking out in a corner of the lab.

The monkey sighed. "Gotta go." He reluctantly turned and lurched toward the commotion.

Rizzo watched the monkey go. The emotional plummet from his entrance to the lab to his exit was immeasurable.

Animal Lab

A few weeks later, the lab was vandalized. No one was hurt, but a lot of equipment was damaged. It was going to be hard to repair, if it could be repaired.

Chapter 28

Charlie had gotten an early start on his chores around the lab. It had taken much getting used to, hearing animals talk. And work. And basically become his boss. It wasn't too bad, though. He liked to stay busy. It kept his mind occupied. And he didn't mind being told what to do, whether by humans or animals. He just liked being useful. The regular sweeping motion kept him calm. It was his meditation. While he swept, he thought of his TV shows and smiled, giggled, or sometimes laughed out loud.

There wasn't much on TV these days except reruns, which was OK with him. He enjoyed the old Warner Brothers cartoons. Bugs Bunny was his favorite. He liked how the "wascally wabbit" always outsmarted his enemies. He also liked the Road Runner who always outsmarted that dumb Wile E. Coyote. Pepé Le Pew didn't do so much for him. He didn't really get why he liked that female cat so much or why she didn't like him. Except that he smelled bad, so he guessed it made sense.

Unfortunately, these cartoons were no longer available. He was told that they denigrated animals and so there were now fines for watching them. At least fines for humans watching them. He didn't understand everything that was going on, but Julius had told him that the legislature had "imposed fines on humans for taking part in anything that denigrated animals." What that meant, Julius explained, was that he shouldn't watch those cartoons anymore. So Charlie found other TV shows to watch, but they just weren't as funny.

Charlie finished cleaning one room, put his cleaning equipment into his cart, and wheeled it into the next room. As he entered, he noticed broken glass on the floor. Some animals had taken to drinking and generally partying after work and he more frequently had to clean up the aftereffects, though usually not broken glass. Charlie sighed and took out his broom and dustpan to begin sweeping. He noticed some spilled wine, not uncommon, so he took out his mop and began mopping the red liquid. As he pushed the mop under a desk, it hit something soft. He heard a low, rumbling noise and pictured a hung-over rabbit or monkey.

"Come on out," Charlie said but got no response. He peered under the table and saw two glowing eyes. It was not a drunken moan that he'd heard but a soft growl. And it was getting louder. The animal was eating something. Watching him. Growling.

Charlie backed up slowly. There was an alarm on the wall, but Charlie had been told not to pull it except in an emergency. Was this an emergency? Was there a difference between an animal emergency and a human emergency? The old rules seemed simple but each new one was more complex than the previous ones and hard for Charlie to understand.

The animal under the table crept out slowly, blood on its fangs and spread around its mouth. The growling grew more ominous. It looked to him like a dog, thin and dirty and scruffy. It bared its blood-soaked teeth, its black eyes staring, unblinking.

The coyote lunged at Charlie who swung at it with his mop, hitting it squarely in the jaw. The coyote flew across the room and started yelping. Charlie pulled the alarm, which rang throughout the lab.

A few monkeys showed up first. They saw Charlie with his broom and the coyote in the corner, wounded. "What did you do?" the monkeys shouted at him.

Charlie stuttered out, "I hit him." As usual, Charlie answered questions briefly and without explanation.

More animals started showing up.

"What happened here?"

The monkeys replied, "He attacked the coyote."

Charlie was simply frozen. In shock from the attack, he was frozen by the inundation of questions and exclamations that he just couldn't process.

"Why did he attack it?"

"Can we trust him?"

"Where did it come from?"

"The human?"

"The coyote?"

"Is it dead?"

"Look at all the blood!"

"Why did he do it?"

"Why? Because he's human!"

His eyes closed, Charlie hadn't noticed the animals closing in on him. The monkeys started grabbing at him, and he tried swatting them away. The mice and rats jumped on him and began biting. Charlie fell to the ground, curled into a fetal position. That allowed other animals to get into the attack, biting, scratching, clawing. Charlie curled tighter, not saying a word. His body started convulsing. From pain or from crying or from some medical condition, the animals didn't know, if they had noticed in the first place.

Julius arrived at the scene, at first confused by the writhing lump of animals. Then he saw a sneaker. A human sneaker. And the mop on the floor. He began tearing animals off of Charlie and flinging them across the room. When the largest ones were off, he straddled Charlie and let out a roar that frightened the other animals away. He bent over and saw Charlie's bleeding form. "My god," he said softly, with tears flowing. He gently picked up Charlie and carried him to the infirmary.

The coyote had been frail from malnutrition to begin with. Charlie's blow had cracked its skull. It was only after Charlie had been taken away and the crowd had cleared that someone noticed the coyote had stopped its yelping and was motionless. It had died.

Chapter 29

Justice Room had again been turned into a courtroom. There was a table for the judge, a table for the defense, a table for the prosecution, chairs for the jurors, and benches for the observers in the galley. Unlike all the other rooms, this one was dark, the walls having been painted a somber brown. The tables, too, were painted to resemble a dark wood though they were manufactured from bright white plastic laminate like everything else in the lab. The jury chairs were painted brown and covered in soft artificial fur of some kind. The benches were painted the same brown color but without the soft padding, almost certainly done on purpose to keep observers from getting too comfortable and turning the trial into entertainment. The whole atmosphere seemed different—more formal, more somber—than the earlier trial of Milagra.

The crowd overflowed the galley and spilled into the hallway. The trial was being broadcast, but most animals wanted a live view.

Arnold presided over the courtroom at the far end, away from the door. To his left were Charlie and Charlie's attorney, a pig named Sunshine. Sunshine kept leaning into Charlie and snorting softly. Charlie stared straight ahead, simply nodding or shaking his head from time to time.

To Arnold's right was Cagney with a frog named Strawberry. They huddled over notes, alternately squeaking and croaking, pointing at various words on the pages, mostly nodding in agreement.

Rizzo sat in the gallery. He had no official role in the trial, but he knew that the consequences were serious and so he should attend the entire thing.

Arnold cleared his throat, which was a surprisingly loud sound, and called the court to order. The animals quieted. "We will first hear from the prosecution."

Cagney and Strawberry continued to pore over their notes, seemingly oblivious to everything around them. Seemingly. This had been rehearsed to give the impression that they were so lost in their work, so determined to bring justice to an unjust world, that nothing else seeped into their brains.

"Mr. Cagney?" said Arnold, more of a statement than a question.

"Oh, yes, your honor," said Cagney. "Just going over a few last-minute details." Cagney got up and saw Billie in the gallery staring intently at him as if to broadcast her thoughts into her head. He smiled at her momentarily, but if she saw it, she had no reaction.

Cagney jumped onto the table and scrambled to the side facing the jury, his whiskers twitching with nervous excitement. "Members of the jury," he started. "You are going to find out about a horrific crime against one of our own. You may hear from the defendant that the victim is an outsider. That the victim, is not one of us. That the victim is illegal. Let me be clear from the outset." He paused dramatically. "None of us is illegal!"

A bleating came from the back. A small group of sheep had moved from out in the hallway into the room, stepping over the smaller animals and squeezing past the larger animals. "No animal is illegal," they bleated over and over until Arnold told them to be quiet or be ejected from the court. Two large chimpanzees made their way toward the sheep, but they stopped their bleating.

Rizzo turned to look at the sheep, surprised. He couldn't even remember sheep in the lab. Were they from the lab or outsiders? He should know, but the legislature had taken on the job of keeping track of animals. Maybe he should have paid closer attention, but it seemed like a simple counting effort that didn't require his oversight. He made a mental note to go back over the records to see who had counted sheep.

Cagney continued. "Some would have you think that humans are worthy of legal protection while some animals are not. That somehow a human could be valued more highly than an animal. But let us not forget the days before Day 1! The days when humans mistreated us. When they experimented on us." Then in a lower pitch, adding a dangerous tone, "When they murdered us."

The sheep began bleating again, "Human murderers, human murderers," over and over, riling up the other animals in the gallery who began to join in.

"I object!" shouted Sunshine from the defendant's table. Charlie, next to him, seemed dejected. It wasn't clear if he was hearing what was happening around him. Or understanding.

"Quiet" roared Arnold. Few had ever heard him raise his voice to such a decibel. The sheep stopped their bleating. "I will not have these interruptions." He turned to Sunshine. "Objection overruled," he said. Then more quietly to Sunshine, "Our rules allow opening statements without restriction. When we get to the evidentiary part of the trial, each party's arguments will be restricted to relevant matters. But for now, everything is fair game."

Cagney nodded at the judge, then turned back to the jury. "This case is not just about that human over there." He did not turn to Charlie but kept gazing at the jury. "It is about whether all animals have rights and whether we will once again let humans take those rights from us. This is a trial about fundamental values of our society. Will we become a society of fairness and justice for all animals?" He then turned ominously toward Charlie. "Or will we once again put ourselves at the mercy of, under the subjugation of, humans?" He paused and continued looking at Charlie for a drawn-out moment. The room was silent. Then he jumped back into his seat as the sounds of agreement could be heard in quiet whispers throughout the courtroom.

Arnold cleared his throat again. "And now we will hear from the defendant."

Sunshine climbed onto the top of the defendant's table and stood on his hind legs to face the jury. This is a trick he'd been practicing to peer above the crowd and stand out in the court, and he had gotten good at it. However, it may have been a bad choice in hindsight, given what this case was about and how animals in general felt about other two-legged animals.

"Animals of the jury," he started out. "I'm here to represent a man…" there was a soft cacophony of noises from the gallery. "Yes, a human," said Sunshine louder. "Let's just be honest here," he said with a slight Southern drawl. "Many of you… well, most of you don't like humans." The was a wave of affirmative noises and nodding of heads. "We know what kinds of things they did to us." More affirmative noises and nodding of heads. "There was mistreatment. Experimentation. Torture. Murder." At each word, the rumbling of the crowd grew. He was getting them worked up.

"Order!" shouted Arnold. The crowd went silent.

Sunshine paused, then resumed softly. "And yet Charlie here…" He pointed slowly to Charlie. "Has done none of these things. Charlie has been kind. Charlie has taken care of us. Charlie was a good man before Day 1 and has been a good man after Day 1. We must not…" He paused and looked around the courtroom. "We must not," he began again, "allow our judgment to be clouded, to be influenced, to be prejudiced by how we feel about his species."

Sunshine paused to take a drink of water from a glass on the table. "We are not here to try all of humankind!" he barked out. Then quietly, "We are here to try Charlie." He turned to Charlie. "Our friend. Charlie."

Sunshine looked at the jury, taking the time to look each one directly in the eyes. "When we get to the heart of this trial, the prosecution must show you evidence of a crime. And if they are able to do that, then they must show you evidence that Charlie committed this crime." Sunshine turned and motioned at Cagney and Strawberry, who had been staring at him, motionless, during his opening argument.

"They will use your feelings about humans against Charlie. You must not be swayed. That is not why we're here. We can deal with the treachery, the deceit of humans some other time. In some other way. But not here. Not now. In a court of law, all animals are treated fairly." "All animals," he repeated, emphasizing the word "all."

"The prosecution must show evidence. Not conjecture. Not assumptions. Not hypotheses. They must show evidence of a crime beyond a reasonable doubt. Evidence that Charlie committed this crime. Beyond a reasonable doubt." He turned to the observers. "But they cannot do that." He turned back to the jury. "And so you cannot convict. Regardless of how you feel. You cannot convict on soft feelings. Only hard facts. And the facts, as I will show, are not there."

Sunshine lowered himself back onto four legs and climbed off of the table and onto his chair.

Chapter 30

There wasn't much to the trial. No one saw what happened except Charlie. Animals testified about what they saw after the incident. Many animals testified, which didn't bring any new facts to light but just drilled the scene of the coyote's death into the minds of the jury, which is exactly what the prosecution attorneys wanted. Sunshine wavered on whether to call Charlie to testify. In the end he decided not to. Of course, the prosecution implied that Charlie didn't testify because he was guilty and might slip up and incriminate himself. The truth was that everyone knew that Charlie had killed the coyote, and Charlie had admitted so. The question was only whether it was self-defense. No one knew. No one but Charlie. And Charlie was slow. And nervous. And human. Three strikes. His testimony would not go well, so Sunshine decided against it. When it was the defense's case, he moved right into the closing argument.

Sunshine again climbed onto the top of the defendant's table and stood on his hind legs, facing the jury. He cleared his throat with a high-pitched peep. "Animals of the jury. We all grieve the death of the coyote. We are animals. We are bound by our animality."

He paused to look at each member of the jury, each staring back, each intent on his words. That was good.

"But we must be a society of laws. Since Day 1 we have created this great civilization. Civilization is marked by its adherence to justice, and that justice is codified in laws that are applied equally to all animals. Including human animals. Because if we apply them selectively. If we apply them to some but not others, then what kind of society have we become?"

He paused again to look at each member of the jury. He wanted to connect with each one personally. He wanted each one to believe that he was talking to them individually. He wanted to reach into their hearts more than their minds, and plead for justice for Charlie.

"This means that our justice must apply equally and fully to all within our society. That means that our justice must apply to humans."

He paused again to make eye contact with each member of the jury. He spoke the next words slowly. "Because if not, then we have not learned anything from the mistakes of the humans. Because if not, then we are no better than them. Because if not, we have failed our friend Charlie. And we have failed utterly as a fair and just civilization."

Sunshine looked once again at each and every jurist and paused at each face. Some stared back unreadable, a few nodded, a few looked at the ground. He hoped he had reached enough of them to sway the vote. He lowered himself back onto all fours and walked quietly back to his seat.

For the prosecution, Cagney hopped onto his table and faced the jury, but remained on all fours. He started quietly. "We have shown you the evidence. We have brought you the witnesses. We have heard from the forensics experts. An animal was found brutally beaten to death. A human was found in the room with the animal." He paused to point his nose toward Charlie, sitting, head bowed.

"He does not deny that he murdered the animal. He claims it was self-defense. Think about how ridiculous that is. A human... killing an animal in self-defense." Like Sunshine, he looked directly at each member of the jury. "Think about how many times humans have killed animals.... for experimentation... for sport... for entertainment... for no reason at all." He paused at each phrase, letting it sink in.

Cagney continued. "All animals must be treated fairly. Our laws emphasize that." He pauses. He has become continuously louder, building toward a crescendo. "But. Humans. Are. Not. Animals." He said each word distinctly. The animals in the galleys erupted. Arnold growled a command to be quiet, but Cagney continued to the growing cheers. "Since the beginning, humans have demanded privilege over the animals! It is time to put an end to human privilege once and for all!" The shouts, cheers, and whistles grew loud, and Arnold's voice could no longer be heard over the din. It took about three minutes for the noise to diminish enough that Arnold's shouts for order could be heard, and another 20 seconds for them to be obeyed.

Cagney continued very quietly. "We can understand when an animal kills to eat. To survive. Especially a natural animal. But when a human kills for no reason, that's not acceptable. That must be punished. You must find this human guilty. Nothing else is acceptable."

Cagney walked back to his seat very slowly. Billie, in the gallery began clapping. Others began clapping. Billie began shouting. Others began shouting. The crowd became loud and raucous, and Arnold could not quiet them. At the defense table, if one looked closely at the blank notepad below Charlie's hung head, one would see the lines on the paper blotting from small, silent tears.

Later that day, the guilty verdict was read aloud. Julius took Charlie's arm and led him to his confinement cage, both of their heads bowed, both sets of eyes moist and vision blurry. The crowd parted as they walked together down the hallway, but the angry shouts didn't cease. Anger, it turned out, was a much better motivator than reason.

Chapter 31

"Hey, man" said Julius as he entered the room and encountered Charlie, nude, crouching in a corner of the jail cell, eating a banana. "Where are your clothes?"

"They took 'em away," said Charlie without looking up.

"Why?"

Charlie just shrugged.

"At least they're feeding you."

"If you like bananas."

"As a matter of fact, I do!"

There was a silent pause as Julius fidgeted, thinking of something to say.

"I don't suppose you want to…"

"No," interjected Charlie, cutting him off.

"You didn't hear…"

"No thumb wrestling."

"I wasn't going to say that," lied Julius. "I… just wanted to… say I'm sorry."

"Why?"

"I don't know. Aren't you supposed to say that? To make someone feel better?"

"Just go," said Charlie.

"I thought…"

"Just go!"

Julius hesitated, thinking there was something he could or should say, but nothing came to him. So he turned to go.

"Wait," said Charlie. "I'm sorry. None of this is your fault."

"You shouldn't be sorry. Neither of us should be sorry. We're friends," said Julius. "What can I do for you, man?"

"Can you get me something other than bananas?"

"Sure thing," said Julius. "At least I can try."

"Thanks, monkey," said Charlie, looking up at Julius with a smile, his eyes red and wet.

Julius smiled back, and it was a soft smile. Sincere. He'd been working on it. Then he became serious. "Don't do the monkey thing," he said quietly.

"What monkey thing?"

"We're not supposed to mis-species any animals. Not call any animal by the wrong species. It's a new law. It insults the animals."

"Which animals?"

"I don't know. All the animals, I guess."

"You?"

"Not me. You can call me what you want. I just don't want to get you into any more trouble."

Charlie looked down again at the floor.

Julius thought for a moment. "I can bring you news of the world."

"I don't think I want that," said Charlie.

"You'll want this news. That young girl teacher was asking about you. The pretty one."

"Human girl?"

"Of course."

"Pretty?"

"Yeah. Pretty. If you don't mind hairless face, arms, and legs. And the rest of her, I assume. You like that kind of thing, don't you?"

"Karen?"

"Yeah, that's her. She does have a nice voice. And a nice scent."

"What did she ask about me?" asked Charlie, perking up a little.

"Just things. How are you? if you asked about her."

"She asked that?"

"Yeah. I think so… Yeah."

Charlie perked up a bit more. Then Rizzo came into the room and saw the two of them. "Oh, I'll come back later," he said and turned to go.

"What do you want?" said Julius indignantly.

"To check up on Charlie." He turned back to the cage. "Do you need anything?" Then looking more closely, "Where are your clothes?"

"They took 'em away," said Julius.

"Who?"

Julius shrugged and looked at Charlie.

"I don't know. I was given a break to bathe and when I got back, they were gone."

Rizzo sighed loudly. "I'll get them back."

"You can do that?" asked Charlie.

"I'm the president. Sure... I think so. I'll ask around." Rizzo looked up and down the cage, at Charlie, then at Julius. "I'm really sorry, Charlie. This shouldn't have happened. I'm trying to get you a new trial."

"You can do that?" asked Charlie.

"I'm the president. Of course I can... I think so. I'll find out soon."

"Why is all this happening, Rizzo? Things were good. We all got along. What changed? And why?"

"I don't know, Julius. It doesn't make sense. Things had been getting so much better for a while. We had built a true civilization with rights and responsibilities."

"The Seven Rights and Responsibilities!" chimed Charlie.

"Yes. We were succeeding where even the humans had failed." He looked at Charlie. "No offense, Charlie."

"No, you're right. I felt safer here. For a while."

"I don't know what happened to change that," said Rizzo. "I don't get it. I'm trying to figure it out. Reading more philosophers. More history. There's a lot to catch up on."

At that moment there was an almost imperceptible flutter of wings in the rafters. Rizzo looked up. "Who's up there?"

"Is that Evan up there?" asked Julius, squinting. "Come down or I'll pull you down!"

Evan spread his wings wide and glided down to a tabletop, stretched his wings even wider, and then folded them up again.

"You better not spy on me again," said Julius.

"Nevermore," quote Evan.

"Is that all you can do, Evan?" asked Rizzo. "Quote and mimic? I keep wondering if you went through the same transformation as the rest of us or if you're just repeating phrases you don't understand."

"It's you who doesn't understand," said Evan.

"OK, what don't I understand?" asked Rizzo. He still wasn't sure if Evan was just repeating, just mocking, or actually about to complete a full thought.

"It's about power."

"What is?"

"The division. Maybe it started out as good intentions. But now it's about power."

"How? Why?"

"Setting animals against each other in the name of justice. The ones who are manipulating, pulling the leashes so to speak, are finding that doing so gives them power. It starts out with a sincere intention to bring about justice. But after a while, it becomes something else, and justice is used to rationalize the power grab."

"And how do you know this?"

"I've been watching. I watched the humans, too. It was the same then as it is now."

"So how do we stop it?"

"Find those in power before they become more powerful."

"Who are they?"

"You don't know?"

"Maybe," said Rizzo hesitating. "But I want to hear from you. I've been reading and studying and trying to figure all this out. But you seem to have some special insight. Or you claim you do. So you tell me."

"Those who do not learn history are doomed to repeat it. But also, when your nose is in books, you miss the sights in front of you."

Rizzo was annoyed with Evan's platitudes and hints like one of those soothsayers in a fantasy novel who could give the right advice but then the novel would end. "So what do you think I should do? I just want your advice."

"The presidential elections are coming up, right?" asked Evan rhetorically.

"Yes."

"Well you better know who your enemy is by then and what to do about it."

"My enemy? There are no enemies. There are only differences of opinions."

"Then you have nothing to worry about, do you?" At that, Evan spread his slick black wings and launched into the hallway and out of sight.

Animal Lab

Chapter 32

Charlie's trial had been some time ago, and things had gotten back to normal, if there really was a normal in this new and evolving society of Animerica. Things seemed calm on the surface, but below the surface was an itch that couldn't be scratched. It could be felt, though animals did not talk about it. At least in public.

Cagney had made a name for himself at the trial. He had become a hero, a champion of animal rights. He had thrown his hat into the presidential ring, a challenger to Rizzo. Since the trial, Cagney had traveled the lab talking to people, giving speeches, Billie always at his side.

Rizzo eschewed speeches. He had too much to do. He saw the unrest and it worried him. He was sure the animals would see the success of his programs, he thought. There was no need for shaking hands, kissing babies, or giving speeches. There was too much work to do, and he needed another term to complete it. At least. The animals would see that. They would see how life had improved. He would ask for another term to continue leading, to see his programs to fruition. They would give him another term. He was sure of it.

The legislature decided that there should be a presidential debate between the candidates. That seemed like a good idea to Rizzo. Let the animals hear the candidates, compare their philosophies, look at their achievements, and then decide. Cagney had introduced the proposal in the first place, so it was clear that he was also in favor of a comparison of ideas.

Freedom Auditorium was the location for the presidential debate. Rizzo sat at the right side of a table at the front, while Cagney sat on the left. In the middle was an owl, Szigmond, the moderator. The auditorium was packed, every seat occupied by at least one animal. There was standing room only in the back. The debate was being televised throughout all of Animerica.

Szigmond hoo-hooed loudly to start the debate. "Thank you all for being here," she said. "This is a momentous occasion. A first in Animerican history. Our first presidential debate. We should be very proud of the society we have created. We should be very proud of the government we have put in place. And we should be very proud of the laws we have enacted. And we should be especially proud of the Seven Rights and Responsibilities we have recognized to ensure fairness and justice for all animals. All of this is represented here today in the first presidential debates." The auditorium broke into thunderous applause. It seemed that all of Animerica was applauding.

Szigmond waited for the applause to die down and began the questions. Policies were discussed. Rizzo made statements about the Rights and Responsibilities, about freedoms, about unity. Cagney spoke of similar themes, emphasizing fairness and justice and the brave new world of Animerica. To most of the animals listening, they both sounded pretty much the same. There were differences, though. Rizzo focused on plans and policies. Cagney focused on ideas. Rizzo attacked Cagney as being idealistic but without plans, without concrete solutions. Cagney attacked Rizzo as being detached from the real world, from the daily "trials and tribulations" of the animals. As having already forgotten what it was like to do real work. Rizzo fumed at that. He had been doing essential work, he felt. No different than Cagney, so how did Cagney belittle the clear accomplishments that they had both made. Together. Though Rizzo really felt he had done more of the work to build this brave new world.

Then the debate was steered toward specific issues. Rizzo accused Cagney of being soft on immigration. There was a need, Rizzo insisted, to integrate wild animals into society. To educate them or risk the deterioration of this new civilization. Cagney said that it was Rizzo who risked the future of Animerica by treating naturals differently than the other animals. "We are all one!" said Cagney to shouts of agreement.

Yet when it came to justice, Cagney claimed that different species required different treatment to compensate for prejudice and intolerance. "You said we are all one," said Rizzo, "and yet you insist on treating each species differently."

"You're confused, Rizzo," said Cagney condescendingly. "We are all one, yet we are all different and so to achieve unity, we must raise up those who have been mistreated."

"And bring down others?" asked Rizzo.

"We must raise up everyone, but especially the unempowered and disenfranchised!" answered Cagney.

This had no logic, thought Rizzo, but the crowd loved it. Maybe each one saw themselves as disadvantaged and so each one thought Cagney was going to help them more than the others. For the first time, Rizzo clearly realized that for all of his genius with policies and all of his vision about society, he truly lacked an understand of the animal psyche. And for the first time, he realized that Animerica was more fragile than he knew. And it actually scared him.

When the questions of the debate had been exhausted, Szigmond hoo-hooed again loudly to announce the closing arguments.

Cagney walked over to the edge of the table, closer to the audience. He actually seemed nervous. He looked at Billie, who smiled at him and then nodded. He didn't speak. She continued to smile, and nodded a bit more vigorously, a little impatiently.

"Welcome tonight to this munificent event in our country's history. We… we…" He looked around at the very large crowd, each animal starting intently at him in anticipation. He swallowed. "We are here to decide which of us is the best candidate to lead this great country. Which one of us is more qualified to take us in the right direction. Which one has shown a dedication to fairness for all animals. Which one has made an effort to destroy the kinds of privilege that existed before Day 1 and should never exist afterwards!" The crowd erupted in approval. Cagney looked around the auditorium, nodding. He could make out Billie, smiling, nearly bursting.

Cagney looked over at Rizzo, who was looking down at his notes. "Rizzo is a fine rat," he said. "A very fine rat." He paused. "But I have not come to praise Rizzo, I have come to bury him!" Rizzo looked over at Cagney with an expression of shock. In that instant, the crowd became absolutely silent.

Cagney looked shaken, but turned back to the audience and continued. "To bury his administration. To bury his political ideology that he has taken from the humans and tried to apply to us. To animals. We must bury human philosophy in the dustbin of history. We have made a great foundation for a new society, but now we must build upon that foundation to create a house full of fairness. Full of justice! Full of new values, not old values! Full of animal values, not human values!" The crowd broke into a loud cheer.

"Where every animal will live a full life! Where no animal has less than any other animal! Where we stand not for equality of opportunity, a system that humans tried and failed, but a system of equality of outcome. Where each animal lives its life to perfection. Isn't that what we should strive for? A perfect utopia? And I say it's possible!"

Cagney turned back to Rizzo. "But he says, such a world is not possible."

Cagney turned back to the audience. "And what do you say?" Cheers once again broke out throughout the auditorium. Throughout Animerica. He turned and walked slowly, deliberately back to his side of the table. It took a while for the cheers to die down.

"Your turn," hooted Szigmond to Rizzo.

Rizzo looked up from his notes. He realized that he had underestimated Cagney. And Billie. He still hoped that reason would prevail.

Rizzo cleared his throat. "My fellow animals. Thank you for coming out to hear, and to participate in this all so important event. We are all participants in this grand experiment in which we are creating a new civilization. One that strives to be fair, with liberty and justice for all.

"But what do we mean by liberty and justice? Liberty means each animal is in charge of his or her own life. Each of us controls how we ourselves live. The government ensures that we all are allowed our rights and we all live up to our responsibilities as defined in the Seven Rights and Responsibilities. That no one of us interferes with the rights and responsibilities of the others. We have no masters!" The animals broke into applause and cheers.

"The government is not our master!" The applaud grew louder.

"Animals have no human masters!" The cheering grew throughout the entire lab.

"And humans have no animal masters!" The cheering died down. Animals looked at each other confused.

"Because that is fairness," said Rizzo. "Fairness is liberty for all. Because when we start applying liberty to some and not to all, then we have abandoned fairness."

"And what about the naturals!" shouted someone from the audience. "Why do you deny liberty for them? How is that fair?"

Rizzo looked around to find the voice, but couldn't determine its location.

"And what about the Wilds that have been coming into our society?" shouted another animal.

"Naturals," shouted another voice from the audience. "Not wild! Natural!"

Rizzo ignored the voices and continued. "That brings me to justice. Justice means a set of rules so that our society can flourish. That we can resolve problems. That we can resolve disagreements in the least disruptive ways possible. And that we can punish those who would interfere with our rights and responsibilities.

"And fairness means applying our laws equally to all: animals, humans, and wild animals. That means that those who do not understand our laws must be taught them and acknowledge them before we allow them to become full members of our society. It means that we must make an effort to teach them. But they must also make an effort to learn. And any animal that breaks our laws, whether from the lab or from the outside, must suffer the publishment. Our society cannot survive if pleading ignorance to our laws avoids punishment for breaking them."

The crowd started murmuring, the murmuring grew louder, some smattering of applause began and traveled throughout the auditorium and into the hallways. Then, from the back of the room, there was a bleating that grew louder. Rizzo squinted and could barely make out a number of sheep in the back of the auditorium, moving very slowly toward the front. They were bleating, "All animals are equal and if not, we must make them equal!"

Some in the crowd started chanting with the sheep. Others started joining in. Cagney got up and began waving his arms to lead the crowd in the chanting.

"I'm not done!" shouted Rizzo, but he couldn't be heard over the growing chants.

"All animals are equal and if not, we must make them equal!"

Szigmond was hooting for silence, but no one could hear her.

Cagney moved closer to Rizzo. "What do you think," he shouted at Rizzo sarcastically.

Rizzo fumed, shouted back at Cagney, "I have my right to speak. I demand my right to speak."

Cagney responded, "You have your right to speak. And they have theirs. They just happen to speak louder."

Chapter 33

The votes were cast and counted. Cagney won the presidency.

His inauguration took place in Freedom Auditorium, decorated with patriotic colors, with flags strewn on all the walls. The packed crowd waved their own flags, while those who couldn't fit into the room or the overflowing hallways huddled around monitors throughout Animerica to watch the broadcast.

Cagney and Rizzo stood on either side of the main podium. Julius stood next to the podium at Rizzo's side. Billie stood on the podium with Cagney. Behind them were an eclectic group of animals, all in white lab coats. Arnold, in the middle of the podium, presided over the ceremony.

At Arnold's indication, Rizzo walked solemnly to the center. Cagney took a few skipping steps before catching himself and slowing to a formal stroll.

"Please shake hands," instructed Arnold.

The two rats came together, Cagney smiling giddily, Rizzo serious. They shook hands briefly. Very briefly.

"I now officially mark the transfer of the presidency and all of its rights and responsibilities from Rizzo to Cagney." He turned toward Rizzo. "Thank you for your invaluable service." Rizzo nodded solemnly.

Arnold then turned toward Cagney. "May you preside over this nation with liberty and justice for all."

Cagney smiled and turned toward the crowd. "And fairness!" The crowd erupted.

Rizzo returned to his side of the platform. Julius whispered something to him, and he nodded. Arnold walked toward Rizzo's side, where Julius assisted him off of the platform. Cagney remained in the center and addressed the crowd.

"Thanks for voting me in!" he said to more raucous applause. "Voting for fairness!" Cagney stood on his hind legs and clasped his raised hands in the air in a sign of victory. This was followed by more applause and shouting.

Cagney basked in it, doing nothing to curtail it. He waited for several minutes for it to die down completely, then fell back onto all fours.

"We have much to do," he said, "to correct the injustices of the past." Again there was applause and shouting, but it didn't last as long this time. He waited.

"As a first step, we must distance ourselves from human science. Human science was cruel. It was biased. It was unfair!" There was a smattering of applause and shouts as the animals waited for more. For an explanation.

"The scientists you see behind me…" He waived toward the animals in white lab coats. "These animals are committed to a new animal science. They are committed to a science that is fair. A science that is not cruel. A science that is different than the old science, the science of humans." Wild applause and shouting broke out again. Cagney again waited for it to die out.

"These priests have been hand selected by me, by our beloved Billie, and by those who desire fairness over all else." There was a murmuring, but not the applause and shouting he had expected.

Billie walked over to him, cupped her hands to his ear, and whispered something. "I did not!" he exclaimed, his microphone still live.

Cagney looked back at the crowd, a little hesitant now. He cleared his throat nervously. "These scientists will guide our endeavors to make certain that we are all abiding by the scientific consensus. We cannot have people spreading misinformation. In particular, we cannot have so-called scientists, particularly humanist scientists, spreading information that goes against the scientific consensus. It will not be tolerated!

"For example, we all know, and research has shown this to be true, that animals are superior in nature to humans because humans kill for enjoyment while animals only kill out of necessity. Any statement to the contrary is just not supported by the scientific facts, and we must be a society built on scientific facts. Because science equals fairness."

There was applause and shouting again, but at this point many in the audience were confused. But what mattered to them most, was that they now had a president who understood their issues. Understood their grievances.

Understood that fairness meant giving them what was rightfully theirs and protecting them from those who would deny them these things.

"Along these lines," continued President Cagney, "I have allocated a large budget to the study of Critical Species Theory. This is the study of how certain species have been oppressed over the years, not only by humans but also by members of other species. We do this scientific study so that we can scientifically understand it and use science to discover ways of correcting it. And for achieving fairness."

The crowd erupted once again. Of course, each one thought, President Cagney understands me and my species, and the difficulties that we have endured. He will fix it. He will bring equality. And equity. And fairness. And all will be good.

Chapter 34

Julius paced nervously in the hallway outside the door marked "Office of Fairness." He had come about 10 minutes early but had been pacing for about 20. He finally pushed on the door slowly, peered inside the room, and entered. It was unlike any other room in the lab. It was furnished with rosewood cabinets, a mahogany desk, serious artwork on the walls, and carpeting. Carpeting! Julius had never seen or felt carpeting. It had some kind of instinctual calming feeling against his feet.

Along one long wall were shelves of books. He walked over to them and skimmed the titles. There were manifestos and rulebooks and guides and treatises. Did she ever read anything fun, he wondered? Like *Tarzan of the Apes*? Or *Planet of the Apes*? Or *Congo*?

A side door to the office opened and Julius jumped backward into the bookshelves, rattling the books. Billie entered, but what shocked him in particular was a large coyote at her side, grey and scraggly, baring its teeth. It crossed his mind that the coyote could be making a poor attempt at a smile, just as he had done for so long until he got the hang of it, but that notion was dispelled when a soft but fearsome growl escaped from between the clenched teeth.

"What are you doing in my office?" asked Billie.

"We had an appointment this morning. You called me in."

Billie thought for a minute. "Today?" She thought a bit more. "I'm sure I said tomorrow."

"I remember today," said Julius hesitantly, looking at the coyote who kept its eyes locked on him.

"No, I said tomorrow," said Billie calmly. "Have you learned to tell time yet? We have classes for all the animals."

"I know how to tell time," said Julius indignantly but softly, his eyes darting between Billie and the coyote.

"No matter," said Billie, sighing. "We can talk now. Sit down" She waved to a cushioned leather chair and took her place on top of her desk. The coyote stayed at the side of her desk, its eyes still intent on Julius.

Julius lowered himself into the comfortable chair, another first for him, keeping his eyes on the coyote. He wanted to enjoy the luxury of the chair, but couldn't concentrate on anything but the coyote and its black, unblinking eyes.

Billie finally took notice of Julius' focus on the coyote. "He's a friend," she said. "These days, with all of the trouble, I need protection from extremists. It helps to have him around." She saw that Julius still was focused on the coyote. "Don't mind him. Ignore him. He won't disturb us." Then she added, "If you don't cause trouble."

"What kind of trouble is there here in Animerica? I think we have it pretty good."

"Murders. You think that's 'pretty good'?" she asked mockingly. "Not just murders, we have intolerance. We're doing all we can to suppress it, but like… what's that game? Whack-a-man. The more we try to whack down intolerance somewhere, it pops up somewhere else. It seems to be a never-ending problem." Thinking about what she said, she added, "But we'll end it. It's a matter of perseverance. We need to be more vigilant than the vigilantes. More extreme than the extremists. Achieving fairness is a lifetime's goal, or even an obsession, unfortunately. But one worth pursuing."

Julius slowly brought his eyes off the coyote as Billie spoke and was able to look at her, but kept the coyote in his peripheral vision. "I don't know what this has to do with me," he said.

"We've had reports. Multiple reports. About your behavior."

"I'm just a happy-go-lucky guy."

"See what you just did?"

Julius hesitated. He felt like a scolded child who didn't know what he'd done wrong but was about to find out. After some silence, he realized that she actually wanted an answer. "No," he said meekly.

"You used the term 'guy.' That's a Day Zero term for humans. We don't use human-centric terminology. Do you remember the horrors imposed on animals by humans? Or maybe as an ape, you didn't suffer like the other animals. Were you a pet? A colleague? Do you need to be educated? Reeducated?"

"No. I…"

"You brag about your opposable thumbs as if other animals didn't have their own advantages. As if you and your species are superior to others."

"I'm just proud…"

"Pride is a human fallacy. Pride pits one animal against another whereas we are striving for a society that is equal in every conceivable way. Taking pride is wrong. It hurts society. Do you understand that?"

"I guess I need to think about that…"

"There's no thinking about right and wrong. You need to know it and not waver. We can't tolerate those who will question right and wrong. Do you understand that?"

The coyote started growling as Billie raised her voice, its eyes still riveted on Julius. Julius glanced at the coyote, then back at Billie.

"And you are friends with a convicted criminal."

"Charlie is my friend," said Julius indignantly, standing up suddenly. The coyote took a step toward him, the growling suddenly much louder.

"I suggest you moderate your threatening behavior," exclaimed Billie, "and sit down right now!"

Julius sat down slowly.

"Finally," she continued, "you must stop denigrating other animals."

"Denigrating?"

"You don't know what the word means?"

"I know what it means. I don't know what you mean."

"Don't refer to yourself as a monkey. You're not. Don't belittle the other animals. Don't refer to them by their species. Don't do tasks reserved for other animals. There's a whole list. Too long to explain right now."

"But if I don't know what I'm doing wrong."

Billie stood up on her hind legs. "Mainly, stop gathering with humans. With despicables. Their own kind recognized their issues. That's what destroyed them and their society. We will not repeat that here. We will stop that kind of deterioration before it begins. So you will stop fraternizing with humans."

Julius looked at her, angry, but containing himself. Barely.

"And you will be enrolled in one of our anti-discrimination educational program. Starting tomorrow. I will have you assigned, and you will pick up the appropriate papers at the Office of Education later today."

Julius felt his fists curling into tight balls. Very tight. His eyes watered and the flesh behind the dark hair of his face reddened. But he said nothing.

Billie came down slowly onto all four feet again. "That's all. You can leave." She hopped off the desk and to the side of the coyote. Julius closed his eyes and counted slowly, as he'd learned to do. He stood up slowly, leaned his face toward Billie and the coyote on the floor. The coyote growled, but Julius did not back up this time. He swallowed and began to say something, but then he didn't. He turned around and walked out, fully upright.

Chapter 35

"They make me uncomfortable."

"They shouldn't. You shouldn't even say that."

"I'm just saying the truth."

"The truth can be hurtful."

"But it's the truth."

Billie looked at Cagney, then sank her teeth into his hand. He let out a squeal. "What the hell?"

"When you're civilized, you don't do things that hurt others just because you can."

Billie went back to feeding the coyotes. They gathered around her, playfully taking food from her hands. Such a contrast to the fierce beasts they could become at a moment's notice.

Cagney nursed his hand. He looked around at the luxurious presidential suite that he shared with Billie. Not officially, but their relationship had grown, and she had moved in with him. And decorated for him. "The president," she had said, "must have a presidential suite." He was actually fine with his modest quarters. He didn't really require much. But Billie pointed out that appearances were important. The animals needed to have someone to look up to, to respect and admire. And it needed to be clear that their enemies knew that they were the ones in charge. She used the term "enemies" a lot these days.

"There's been more protests lately," said Cagney.

"I know. You think I'm not on top of that? You think I'm not aware of what's going on in my own country?"

"I just mean that it worries me."

"It worries me too." She looked up from feeding the coyotes as they wandered back to a corner of the room and lay down for a nap. "It's a remnant of Rizzo's time in charge."

"I know," said Cagney hesitantly. "I know… but explain it to me again. It was mostly peaceful while Rizzo was in charge."

"The seeds were planted while he was in charge," she snapped.

"I know, I know," he said. He really did try hard to understand. "But why are things getting worse now."

Billie sighed. "Sometimes I think you don't have the capacity to understand this. Or retain it. I sometimes think that maybe on Day 1 your evolution was retarded for some reason. It's so simple, but you keep wanting me to explain it over and over."

"I know," said Cagney. "I'm not as smart as you. But if you need to explain it to our citizens, you may as well practice on me." Cagney gave Billie a shy smile.

"Yes, you're right," she replied. "You're right. I shouldn't be so hard on you."

"I'm the president," said Cagney with the same subservient smile.

Billie started her lecture. "Under Rizzo's term, hatred and jealousy remained hidden beneath the surface. Animals seemed to be getting along fine, but not really. There was envy and resentment. Some animals took on tasks and excluded other animals."

"Tasks they were better suited at."

"Regardless!" snapped Billie. "Who's to say which animal is 'better' at which tasks?" She made air quotes around the word "better." "All animals are equal and where there is not equality, it is our job to correct it. Otherwise animals grow resentful, especially of other species. So it's our job to suppress that resentment. To make all animals feel equal."

"By making things unequal."

"Exactly! It's like if a table is tilted, you must gnaw away at the longer legs to make the legs equal, to make the table level once more. We're leveling the table upon which our society is built."

"OK," said Cagney. "But now there are protests and work stoppages and growing crime. I'm afraid I'm not succeeding. I'm afraid that things were better under Rizzo."

"Never say that! We're bringing about fairness! Nothing is better than fairness!"

Cagney shrunk back from her a little, like a chastised child.

Billie grew quieter and used her comforting voice. "It's like... It's like... a leaking water pipe. A rusty, leaking water pipe where the water is drip, drip, dripping out of a small hole. As the water flows through it, more water leaks out. But if you don't know to look under the sink, you never see it until one day the kitchen is flooded because the pipe has burst. Under Rizzo's presidency, the pipe was leaking. I could see it, but most people couldn't. Unless I pointed it out to them. There was a constant drip, drip, dripping of speciesism. That's why I insisted you run for president. We had to stop it. So many others just couldn't see it. Until I pointed it out to them. And now we have the power to fix it. But the hole in the pipe is very large, so it will take a while to fix it. We have to keep trying. It seems like it's getting worse, but it's not. You're fixing it."

Billie walked over to Cagney and kissed him gently. "Don't doubt yourself," she said. "You're fixing the leak." She smiled at him. "After all, she said, there's nothing worse than a drowned rat." The two of them giggled.

Chapter 36

Rizzo was making the rounds, surveying the lab, talking to animals. His presidency was over, and he held no official position, but he still took the responsibility of creating a perfect society seriously. As should every animal, he thought.

It was painful though, to pass by lab room after lab room and see various degrees of disarray. There were work stoppages, protests, rivalries. There were murders. He had held out hope that there would be no murders—something that human society was infamous for. He knew that was an unrealistic goal, especially since pre-Day 1, animals had killed each other, but most often for nourishment. The farms, he thought, would bring plentiful food for all, eliminating all killing. But that didn't happen. It did for a while, but then the disagreements and despair came eventually.

Rizzo knew there would be growing pains, of course. Every society had them, from what he'd read. And every society had eventually collapsed under the weight of them. He thought he could study them and avoid the pitfalls, but he hadn't succeeded.

Cagney didn't help. Or more accurately, Billie didn't help. No, more accurately, Billie hurt things. Accelerated the decline. She meant well. Or did she? Rizzo always felt that Billie was sincere in her belief in fairness, but now it was hard to tell. She had power. The power to change things. And though those changes had made life much worse for the animals in Animerica, she seemed not to see it. Or she saw it and continued to think that her misguided policies would change things for the better. Like driving a car for the first time, applying pressure to one of the pedals you're sure is the brake, and when the car takes off, pressing even harder while ignoring the increasing speed. And the truck in the intersection ahead. Because you just knew that the pedal you were pressing is the brake.

Rizzo came to the lab that housed his Inspiration Project. He walked in, but it was silent. Empty. The project had eventually been cancelled by Billie. Officially by Cagney. The project had fallen into disregard and disrepair shortly after Rizzo left office. The project was initially prestigious. Animals competed to work there and those who were accepted were respected and honored. But then Billie's fairness principles took effect and animals were given positions according to quotas and exceptions and factors other than merit. When animals saw other animals getting accepted who were less qualified, demonstrations broke out. Protests that started peacefully soon became violent. The lab started getting vandalized while Rizzo was still in office, but it became worse after he left. And Cagney and Billie really didn't want Rizzo to have a legacy. They saw him as a founding parent of Animerica and didn't erase his name from the history books exactly, but they felt that he was going down the same path that destroyed human society and didn't want animals following him. So they minimized most of what he had done and made it clear that they were correcting his mistakes.

Rizzo sighed. He had begun to think of everything happening as the 'D's: disregard, despair, disrepair, disappointment. And eventually destruction. He curled up in a corner and cried.

Lost in despair, he didn't hear the sound. It was very soft. But he should have heard it. Then a soft rattle, but he couldn't miss that. He jerked his head up to see a large rattle snake sitting not far from him. Coiled. Within striking distance. It eyed him, its head in the air, swaying ever so slightly. The rattle going softly, but getting stronger slowly.

"Who are you?" Rizzo asked. He didn't remember any snakes in the lab. He should know, but Billie had blocked his proposed census. Speciesist, she had claimed.

"Can I help you?" asked Rizzo, though he knew the snake was probably not vocal. Almost certainly a Wild. He held himself taught to keep from shivering, a motion that he felt would attract the snake even more so and might trigger an instinctual strike. But it was difficult, and he could feel a trembling building within.

"Can I help you?" he asked again. He considered his options and there didn't seem to be any. He could try to run, but was certain he could not outrun the snake at this close distance. With that thought, the shiver building inside of him came to the surface. His tail started twitching. He legs started shaking. His whiskers started vibrating.

The coiled snake struck out. It reached Rizzo's face, and he saw into the gaping, fanged abyss.

A large black hand appeared and swatted the snake away. "Run," shouted Julius, and Rizzo took off until he was a safe distance to observe. The snake struck again and lodged its fangs into Julius' arm. Julius gave out a howl. He grasped the snake in his hands while its fangs were still embedded in his arm. The rattle was going off wildly. Julius began swinging his arm over his head. The snake's tail thrashed through the air, but its head remained embedded in Julius' arm, injecting its venom into his bloodstream. Julius continued to howl, but his movements became slower. His arms appeared heavier. His body seemed more massive. He pirouetted slowly, like a ribbon dancer. A deathly ribbon dancer. Julius' footing began to falter. His legs began to crumble underneath him. His body started to fall to the ground, seemingly in slow motion to Rizzo's eyes.

Julius fell, slowly, as though underwater. The venom spread throughout his body. All his muscles began to contract. He took one deep breath, the air filling his lungs but at the same time burning them. Then he exhaled and, while doing so, brought the tail of the snake down hard—as hard as he possibly could—onto the edge of a table.

Julius hit the ground hard. There was a loud cracking sound. Blood spewed across the floor, across the table, onto the walls, and even a spattering on the ceiling. Julius lay sprawled on the floor, breathing slowly. Very slowly. The snake had dislodged from his arm and lay beside him, in two distinct pieces held together by a thin piece of scaly skin.

Rizzo rushed over to him. He then heard a sound behind him, in the doorway of the lab. He turned to see Cagney.

"I'll get help," said Cagney, and ran out of the room.

Moments later, a team of monkeys came in and took Julius to the medical facility, Rizzo running behind.

Chapter 37

Rizzo sat in his small residence, plainly decorated with a few scattered photographs on the walls. His head lay on the tiny table in front of him, a thimble-sized bottle of whisky next to him. There was a flutter of wings at the entrance, which drew his attention in time to see a great span of black feathers covering the doorway, suddenly contracting into the form of Evan who walked slowly through the doorway, each step perfectly timed like a metronome, his body swaying with each footstep. He said nothing.

"You don't wait to be invited in?" asked Rizzo.

Evan kept walking slowly until his belly gently touched the other side of the table. "Everything starts out equal."

"So you've come here to spout cryptic phrases?"

"Everything starts out equal," repeated Evan.

"Thank you," said Rizzo. "I don't know what it means or why it matters. I do know it's wrong. But thank you."

"You can't solve the problem because you don't understand the problem."

"And so 'everything starts out equal' is the problem?"

"Yes."

"Well then, I now understand the problem. Thank you. I'll start working on the solution."

Evan stood still staring at Rizzo silently.

"What else?" Rizzo asked, exasperated.

"That's what they believe."

"Who?"

"Cagney. Billie. Their followers."

"Well of course it's nonsense. If that's what they believe, then they're irrational and so there's no solution. You can't rationally solve an irrational problem."

"You can solve a problem that has consistent assumptions and rules. If you know the assumptions and rules. Even if those assumptions and rules are wrong."

Rizzo lifted his head to stare back directly into Evan's eyes. A staring match. Evan didn't blink, and it was unnerving, so he finally turned away. "You're not helping. Thank you for your input. Now I'm going to go back to my drink."

Evan remained silent but didn't move for several minutes while Rizzo attempted to ignore his towering figure.

"OK, can you explain it to me?" Rizzo finally blurted out. "Not catch phrases, but real information? Full sentences?"

Evan started as if he had simply been waiting for the invitation to explain. "Billie and Cagney and their followers—let's call them Progressives---believe that every animal starts out exactly equal to each other animal."

"Well, that's ridiculous."

"Yes, but they believe it. You need to understand their underlying assumptions."

"But how could a rat be equal to… a monkey? A rat is small and flexible and fits in small places. A monkey is large. A rat can run. A monkey can swing. A rat has a highly sensitive sense of smell. A monkey has a prehensile tail."

"You need to know their assumptions and rules. Even if those assumptions are wrong."

"So you're saying they believe that every animal is equal."

"No. They believe that every animal starts out equal."

"OK. How does that help me? How does it help our society?"

"Every animal starts out equal. But not every animal ends up equal. If a thing starts out one way and ends up another way, then some external force has affected it. Changed it."

Rizzo thought for a moment. Was this nonsense? Something felt true, but he still didn't get it. He was wavering between asking for further explanation and just thanking Evan for his "inspiring advice" and asking him to leave.

Evan let out a caw that shook Rizzo. "If some animals are less capable than other animals, if some animals have fewer resources than other animals, if some animals are better educated, wealthier, healthier than other animals, it is only because some external force interfered. Fairness requires that those external forces be controlled, diverted, corrected. To make all animals equal again. Their natural state."

"And that's their philosophy," said Rizzo half asking half answering.

"That is what drives their every decision," replied Evan.

It was starting to make sense after all, thought Rizzo. "And so Billie will promote policies to 're-equalize' all animals."

"Promote policies, yes. Do whatever it takes. In the name of fairness. By any means necessary."

"Any means necessary?"

"Any. Means. Necessary."

"And so what do you suggest I should do?" asked Rizzo.

Evan leaned in, close enough for Rizzo to feel Evan's hot breath on his whiskers. "Remember. By any means necessary. By. Any Means. Necessary." With that, Evan turned around, walking out the door, spread his wings, and flew away.

Chapter 38

One day, Julius disappeared.

He had gone to the infirmary after he rescued Rizzo from the snake. The venom had saturated his bloodstream and the doctors weren't sure how to stop it from killing him. They administered all kinds of drugs, but this was something new for them. Julius went into a coma. The doctors and nurses fed him intravenously. They hooked him up to machinery to monitor his heart and breathing and blood pressure and temperature. And they waited.

Rizzo visited Julius every day, sat by his side for an hour or two, and then left feeling sad. And responsible. But also feeling thankful. It was an emotionally difficult time for Rizzo. Every day, he had prayed for Julius' recovery.

Then after about a week, Julius came out of his coma. It wasn't some dramatic moment between him and Rizzo—not like something out of the movies. It was about 2 or 3 in the morning, Julius woke up, very groggy, and started moaning softly. It was maybe an hour before a nurse making the rounds heard him and came into his room. He whispered that he was "damn thirsty," and she brought him some water. He went back to sleep.

But the next morning he woke up, disoriented among all the beeping and blinking machines. "Hey," he shouted. A nurse came running. "I'd like some breakfast," he said.

Rizzo came by a little later to see Julius and was surprised to see him snacking and watching TV. "Hey," Julius said when he noticed Rizzo standing in the hallway. He couldn't see the tiny tear in Rizzo's eye.

Rizzo came over to Julius's side and jumped onto the chair by his bed. Julius held out his hand and Rizzo climbed into it. "You want to watch?" Julius asked. "It's an old show about a horse that outsmarts the humans it lives with, in particular this guy named Wilbur. It's kind of funny. Not great literature, but…"

Rizzo spent most of the day in Julius' hand watching old TV shows.

After about another week, Julius was strong enough to get out and start physical therapy. He was weak and his legs got wobbly after only a few minutes at first. After another week, he could stand for an hour or so. After a few more weeks, he was probably at about 60% strength all over and was sent home. A few weeks after that, he resumed work. He wanted to start much earlier, but Rizzo insisted that he take more time off to adjust, and just to relax. He got Cagney to agree to the temporary leave extension.

Julius went to visit Charlie when he got out of the hospital. Charlie was increasingly despondent and there wasn't much Julius could do for him. The visits grew less frequent.

Julius started work again, but spent most of the time at his desk. He wanted to do more—go on patrols, investigate crimes—but Cagney told him that his health was too important, and he needed to slow down until he was back at 100%. Instead, Cagney appointed a gorilla named Kong to handle security.

Then one day, Julius disappeared. He didn't show up at work. Rizzo went to his office and found no one there. He asked Kong where Julius was, but Kong just shrugged. Kong could talk, of course, but he rarely chose to do so.

Rizzo went to Julius' living quarters, but it was open and empty. Everything was in place. Or rather everything was where Rizzo expected it to be. Julius was messy, but in a predictable way. Clothes on the floor in a particular corner. Dishes in the sink stacked so high before they started getting washed. Everything was "out of place" but nothing was unusually out of place.

Rizzo went to see Charlie, but Charlie said he hadn't seen Julius in a while. Rizzo was tempted to ask Charlie more questions, but thought that Charlie probably didn't need to hear that his one friend in the world was now missing. Rizzo figured it was more than Charlie would be able to handle.

The next day, when Julius was still missing, Rizzo went to see Cagney who immediately asked Kong to investigate. Kong nodded and went out the door. No plans, no phone calls, just went out the door to start asking questions. That was his way.

Days went by. Then weeks. Julius' disappearance occupied the subject of most of the talk among the animals. Rumors and bizarre stories were spread about crimes and conspiracies, kidnappings and abductions. Kong's investigation seemed to have stalled, though it wasn't clear to Rizzo that it had gotten started in the first place.

The rumors about Julius' disappearance coalesced eventually into a single theory about Julius conspiring with the humans against the animals. Julius was most like the humans, after all, and enjoyed associating with them more than he did with the animals. His best friend was a human murderer, after all. In one version of the rumor, Julius was involved in a plot to take back the lab for the humans, but something went wrong and the humans turned on him, murdering him. In another version, Julius was in hiding because his plot had been discovered and now the humans distrusted him, and the government of Animerica would lock him up if he were found.

Reporters started asking Cagney, and Billie, about the rumors, but they said only that an investigation was under way. They neither confirmed nor denied the rumors which, as the weeks went on, made Rizzo furious. They could easily put these stupid rumors to rest, but instead they fed this irrational fire. Why didn't they just say something? Release the findings of the investigation? It didn't make sense.

Rizzo finally decided to do something. Cagney was planning a state-of-the-nation address to the legislature, the press, and the public. Rizzo would attend.

On the day of the address, Rizzo felt good. And prepared. He walked toward Fairness Auditorium, which had been renamed from Freedom Auditorium, where he could hear Cagney's voice though the door was closed. Cagney was assuring the animals that the nation was heading in the right direction despite some recent bumps in the economy. That the decrease in productivity was a temporary correction of the mistakes of the previous administration. That the increase in crime was an understandable reaction to all of the problems he had inherited from the previous administration. And that most importantly, the programs on fairness and equality were moving ahead smoothly, as planned, and that ending speciesism was just around the corner.

Rizzo got to the double doors that led into the auditorium, but Kong stood guarding it, standing at attention, unblinking, motionless.

"I'm going in to hear the speech," said Rizzo.

"No entry," replied Kong.

"I said I'm going in to hear the speech," said Rizzo.

Kong said nothing but remained rigidly in place.

Rizzo moved forward.

Kong leaned forward, leaning toward Rizzo.

Rizzo was stunned. "I'm the former president!"

Kong was silent.

Rizzo thought for a moment, then backed away and around a corner. It's hard to keep a rodent out of a room. It had been a while, but he still knew how to sniff out small holes and contract his body to fit through small cracks. He was able to find his way in, crawling inside walls, and eventually out near the podium where Cagney was speaking.

"We will root out injustice, destroy unfairness, eliminate prejudice, and correct inequality until all of us are equal as it should be!" proclaimed Cagney.

Rizzo could not wait, knowing that whoever was trying to keep him out of this room could come after him—Kong or whomever was giving Kong orders. Rizzo climbed onto the podium bedside Cagney and turned to face him. "I want to know what happened to Julius!" he screamed.

Cagney backed away, nearly falling off the podium. "Get him out of here!"

"I want to know what happened to my good friend Julius! I have a right to know. The animals of Animerica have a right to know. Release the investigation findings. Stop the foolish rumors. Bring out the truth."

The double doors in the back of the room burst open and Kong came bounding toward the podium. Rizzo scrambled off it onto the floor where he noticed Billie approaching him accompanied by several snarling coyotes. The largest one leaped at him.

Rizzo scrambled under chairs and tried to find small places where he could evade his pursuers. He couldn't outrun them, but he could squeeze into tiny spaces where they couldn't approach. He had to continue to find small spaces and scramble safely from one to the next. Kong was coming from one direction, the coyote from the other. He ran between animals who backed away, mostly confused by what was happening. From a distance, he saw a swollen open seam in a wall. It might be large enough for him to squeeze through. He wasn't sure. But he put every ounce of speed into a sprint toward that crack. He reached it and felt a swipe at his back and then his back became warm. He squeezed through and disappeared into the wall.

Cagney was shaking. Billie looked at him and motioned for him to take the podium again, but his heart was racing, and he couldn't catch his breath. So Billie mounted the podium and spoke to the animals of Animerica. "There are those among us who would try to impede our vision of a perfect society where every animal is treated equally and where fairness reigns. We must be diligent. The enemies may be a neighbor who harbors speciesist tendencies. It may be a relative who has been brought up believing in him or herself above others." She paused and looked at the crack in the wall and the slight smear of blood on the wall beside it. "It may be a leader who has taken us off the path and into an evil direction. Whoever impedes our journey toward righteousness must be stopped." She paused and looked around. "By any means necessary." She looked over the entire crowd. "Because our mission is that important."

A few animals in the crowd began clapping slowly. Others joined in, a few at a time, until the entire auditorium was clapping in unison to a slow beat.

Rizzo was never seen again.

Chapter 39

Billie called an emergency meeting in Equality Room, formerly known as Independence Room. Cagney sat silently by her side. Only a few legislators were allowed. Guards stood at each doorway to keep animals out. A minimal television crew was inside, broadcasting throughout Animerica.

The camera-animal, earphones over its head, counted down, while forcefully rocking his finger at her with each count. "Three! Two! One!"

Billie shuddered unexpectedly with the realization that the finger looked like a gun. Billie had been haunted lately by visions of assassination. That accounted for the very small audience of trusted politicians, and the television crew had been vetted, but who knew how thorough that was? She made a mental note to enhance background checks and create a database to keep tabs on residents. And to make sure to ban weapons of any kind.

"You're on," whispered the camera-animal.

Billie snapped out of her thoughts. "My fellow country-animals. I come here to give you courage and guidance in these trying times." Her throat was dry, so she cleared it with a muffled squeak that took many by surprise. She regretted that it interrupted the cadence she had planned so carefully.

"We have seen an upswing in crime as of late. We have seen attacks by animals of one species against animals of another species. We have seen government officials disappear. And we have, very unfortunately, seen government officials turn against the government and, in doing so, turn against the animals of this great nation."

"This last part saddens me, in particular." She started shaking a bit and a tear dropped from one eye. The TV camera zoomed in on it. She found that it was much easier than she had planned. "Rizzo was one who assisted me in creating this great nation. He deserves our everlasting respect." She paused for effect. "But also our pity. We don't know what has happened to him, and he may still be among us, plotting. We also know that Rizzo had a great number of followers, so we must be wary. We are building a fragile structure of equality among species, and neither the whispers of hateful slurs nor the strong arm of violent protests must be allowed to sway this fragile structure and cause it to fall."

Billie again let out a muffled squeal to clear her throat. "For this reason, I ask all of you to be vigilant. Be on the lookout for hate speech, whether against you or against one of your species. All hate speech can be reported anonymously to my Department of Fairness where the perpetrator will be punished. I give you my word.

"Also, I have ordered the humans to be sequestered. My administration is… President Cagney's administration is right now building separate, guarded housing for humans. We know that their disease of hate was spread by them amongst themselves and also directed at us animals, and it led to their downfall. We cannot let this disease spread to our peaceful nation. We cannot let animals become the victims, or the perpetuators of hate. I will not allow it!

"Finally, I realized that we must make our lives simpler. Simplicity brings bliss. And so in that regard…" Billie turned to where the Seven Rules and Responsibilities had once proudly hung. The camera followed her motion, as planned, to show in its place was a bright neon sign that exclaimed, "Do No Evil."

"After all, there's no need for complicated rules. Fairness does not require rules. Equality does not require rules. Instead we must all simply agree to do no evil. That's what all our rules boil down to. Everything else is just commentary."

Billie again let out a muffled squeal. "I want us to say this in the morning and again at night. I want you to say it when you great someone. I want you to say it before you make a difficult decision. I want it to keep it in mind when you deal with other people, in business, in love, in all animal relationships. "

Billie let out another muffled squeal. "You will know when something is evil," she said. "And if you don't know," she paused a took a long breath, "just ask me. "

There was a silence throughout all of Animerica. An uncomfortable silence. Billie began chanting, "Do no evil. Do no evil."

On cue, a camera panned the room to show others in the small audience joining her in the chant. The camera panned to the back where a small flock of sheep began bleating in synchronicity with her, "Do no evil. Do no evil. Do no evil. Do no evil."

Many animals watching on TV happily joined Billie in her chant. Some refrained, uncertain. Others stood silently until the stares of their fellow animals cut into their hearts and they joined the chant. The chanted words seemed to fill every room and hallway of Animerica. After a while, the words started to sound strange—wrong—like when you repeat a common word over and over and suddenly it sounds unfamiliar.

"Do no evil. Do no evil. Do no evil. Do no evil. Do no evil. Do no evil. Do no evil. Do no evil…"

Do no evil.